S0-CDP-046

"We never got a chance to dance."

A frisson of excitement raced across Kat as she registered the rumble of Rye's words. She let him turn her around, felt his other hand settle on her waist.

Her laughter was as soft as her silken hair. "In case you haven't noticed, I'm not exactly in dancing shape." She waved a hand toward her walking boot.

"I wasn't thinking of anything too strenuous. Not your pliés or arabesques or that sort of thing."

"Mmm," she whispered. "You've been doing your homework."

"All part of renovating the studio. I have to know how the space is going to be used, don't I?" That was a lie, though.

"Ready to sign up for a class?" she asked, obviously amused.

"I don't think either of us needs any training." He pulled her close, relishing her surprised gasp even as she yielded to his pressure.

Dear Reader,

I was an adult when I attended my first professional ballet, *Giselle*. I fell for the romance, hook, line and sinker. When I came home from the theater, I announced that I was going to be a ballerina.

My friends and family laughed. I hadn't exactly been a star when I dropped out of my beginning ballet lessons. I wasn't a vision of grace or coordination. In recognition of my impossible dream, my mother started gifting me with stuffed animals dressed in ballet tutus (a sheep, a cow, a bunny...).

Though I realized I wasn't meant to dance, the romance of that ballet never faded. When I started to imagine life in a small town in Virginia, I realized that I could finally complete my dream (in a way). I could write about a ballerina.

Kat Morehouse can't imagine returning home after the excitement of New York City. Rye Harmon has finally escaped the small town, moving up the road to Richmond. Nevertheless, Kat and Rye find themselves back in Eden Falls.

I've loved building Kat and Rye's life, and I'm thrilled to share Eden Falls with you. I love to hear from my readers—please stop by and visit me at www.mindyklasky.com.

All best wishes,

Mindy

THE DADDY DANCE

MINDY KLASKY

Harlequin®

SPECIAL EDITION

If you purchased this book without a cover you should be aware that this book is stolen property. It was reported as "unsold and destroyed" to the publisher, and neither the author nor the publisher has received any payment for this "stripped book."

Recycling programs
for this product may
not exist in your area.

ISBN-13: 978-0-373-65646-2

THE DADDY DANCE

Copyright © 2012 by Mindy L. Klasky

All rights reserved. Except for use in any review, the reproduction or utilization of this work in whole or in part in any form by any electronic, mechanical or other means, now known or hereafter invented, including xerography, photocopying and recording, or in any information storage or retrieval system, is forbidden without the written permission of the publisher, Harlequin Enterprises Limited, 225 Duncan Mill Road, Don Mills, Ontario M3B 3K9, Canada.

This is a work of fiction. Names, characters, places and incidents are either the product of the author's imagination or are used fictitiously, and any resemblance to actual persons, living or dead, business establishments, events or locales is entirely coincidental.

This edition published by arrangement with Harlequin Books S.A.

For questions and comments about the quality of this book please contact us at Customer_eCare@Harlequin.ca.

® and TM are trademarks of Harlequin Books S.A., used under license. Trademarks indicated with ® are registered in the United States Patent and Trademark Office, the Canadian Trade Marks Office and in other countries.

www.Harlequin.com

Printed in U.S.A.

Books by Mindy Klasky

Harlequin Special Edition

The Mogul's Maybe Marriage #2135
The Daddy Dance #2164

RDI/MIRA Books

Jane Madison series:
Girl's Guide to Witchcraft
Sorcery and the Single Girl
Magic and the Modern Girl

As You Wish series:
How Not To Make a Wish
When Good Wishes Go Bad
To Wish or Not To Wish

MINDY KLASKY

learned to read when her parents shoved a book in her hands and told her that she could travel anywhere in the world through stories. She never forgot that advice. These days, Mindy works and plays in a suburb of Washington, D.C., where she lives with her family. In her spare time, Mindy knits, cooks and tries to tame the endless to-be-read shelf in her home library. You can visit Mindy at her website, www.mindyklasky.com.

To my writers' retreat girlfriends,
who gave Rye his name—
Nancy Hunter, Jeri Smith-Ready,
Maria V. Snyder, and Kristina Watson

Chapter One

Kat Morehouse pushed her sunglasses higher on her nose as the train chugged away from Eden Falls, leaving her behind on the platform. Heat rose in waves off the tiny station's cracked parking lot. Plucking at her silk T-shirt, Kat realized for the first time since she'd left New York that solid black might not be the most comfortable wardrobe for her trip home to Virginia. Not this year. Not during this unseasonably hot spring.

But that was ridiculous. She was a dancer from New York—black was what she wore every day of her life. She wasn't about to buy new clothes just because she was visiting Eden Falls.

Her foot already itched inside her walking boot cast. She resisted the urge to flex her toes, knowing that would only make her injury ache more. Dancer's Fracture, the doctors had grimly diagnosed, brought on by overuse. The only cure was a walking boot and complete rest from ballet for several weeks.

Looking down at her small roller suitcase, Kat grimaced and reminded herself that she wasn't going to be in Eden Falls for very long. Just time enough to help her family a bit—give her mother a little assistance as Susan nursed Kat's father, Mike, who was recovering from a nasty bout of pneumonia. Take care of her niece for a few days while Kat's irresponsible twin sister roamed somewhere off the beaten track. Look in on her mother's dance studio, the Morehouse Dance Academy, where Kat had gotten her start so many years ago. She'd be in Eden Falls for five days. Maybe six. A week at most.

Kat glanced at her watch. She might not live in Eden Falls anymore, but she knew the train schedule by heart, had known it ever since she'd first dreamed of making a life for herself in the big city. The southbound Crescent stopped at one-thirty in the afternoon. The northbound Clipper would churn through at two-fifteen.

Now, it was one forty-five, and Susan Morehouse was nowhere in sight. In fact, there was only one other person standing on the edge of the parking lot, a passenger who had disembarked with Kat. That woman was tall, with broad shoulders that looked like they were made for milking cows or kneading bread dough. Her oval face and regular features looked vaguely familiar, and Kat realized she must be one of the Harmons, the oldest family in Eden Falls.

Shrugging, Kat dug her cell phone out of her purse, resigned to calling home. She tapped the screen and waited for the phone to wake from its electronic slumber. A round icon spun for a few seconds. A minute.

More. The phone finally emitted a faint chirp, dutifully informing her that she was out of range of a recognized cell tower. Out of range of civilization.

Kat rolled her eyes. It was one thing to leave New York City for a week of playing Florence Nightingale in Eden Falls, Virginia. It was another to be cut off without the backbone of modern communications technology. Even *if* Kat was looking forward to helping her mother, a week was really going to stretch out if she didn't have a working smart phone.

Squinting in the bright sunlight, Kat read a message sent by Haley, her roommate back in New York. The text must have come in during the train ride, before Kat had slipped out of range. OMG, said the text. A + S r here. "A," Adam. The boyfriend of three years whom Kat had sent packing one week before, after discovering his side relationship with Selene Johnson. That would be "S," the corp's newest phenom dancer.

Haley had sent another message, five minutes later. 2 gross.

And a third one, five minutes after that. Hands all over.

All over. Right. Kat and Adam were all over. Adam hadn't had the decency to admit what was going on with Selene. Not even when Kat showed him the silk panties she'd found beneath his pillow—panties that *she* had definitely not left behind. Panties that Selene must have intended Kat to find.

Even now, Kat swallowed hard, trying to force her feelings past the raw, empty space in the middle of her chest. She had honestly believed she and Adam were meant for each other. She had thought that he alone *understood* her, believed in all the crazy sacrifices she had to make as a dancer. He was the first guy—the *only* guy—she had ever gotten involved with, the only one who had seemed worth sacrificing some of her carefully allocated time and energy.

How could Kat have been so wrong? In reality, Adam had just been waiting for the next younger, more fit, more flexible dancer to come along. Kat hated herself for every minute she had invested in their broken relationship, every second she had stolen from her true focus: her dancing career. She closed her eyes, and once again she could see that slinky thong in Adam's bed.

"2 gross" was right.

Kat dropped her useless cell phone into her purse and wiped her palms against her jet-black jeans, feeling the afternoon sun shimmer off the denim. At least her hair was up, off her neck in this heat. Small mercy. She started to rummage deep in her bag, digging for her wallet. A place like Eden Falls had to have pay phones somewhere. She could call her mother, figure out where their wires had crossed. Reach out to her cousin Amanda, if she needed to. Amanda was always good for a ride, whenever Kat made one of her rare weekend appearances.

Before she could find a couple of quarters, though, a huge silver pickup truck rolled to a stop in the parking lot. The Harmon woman smiled as she held out her thumb, pretending to hitch a ride. The driver—another Harmon, by the broad set of his shoulders, by his shock of chestnut hair—laughed as he walked around the front of his truck. He gave his sister a bear hug, swinging her around in a circle that swept her feet off the dusty asphalt. The woman whooped and punched at his shoulder, demanding to be set down. The guy obliged, opening the truck's passenger door before he hefted her huge suitcase into the vehicle's gleaming bed.

He was heading back to the driver's side when he noticed Kat. "Hey!" he called across the small lot, shielding his eyes from the sun. "Kat, right? Kat Morehouse?"

Startled by the easy note of recognition in the man's voice, Kat darted a glance to his face, really studying him for the first time. No. It couldn't be. There was no possible way Rye Harmon was the first guy she was seeing, here in Eden Falls. He started to walk toward her, and Kat started to forget the English language.

But those were definitely Rye Harmon's eyes, coal black and warm as a panther's flank. And that was Rye Harmon's smile, generous and kind amid a few days' worth of unshaved stubble. And that was Rye Harmon's hand, strong and sinewy, extended toward her in a common gesture of civil greeting.

Kat's belly completed a fouetté, flipping so rapidly that she could barely catch her breath.

Rye Harmon had played Curly in the high school production of *Oklahoma* the year Kat had left for New York. Kat had still been in middle school, too young to audition for the musical. Nevertheless, the high school drama teacher had actually recruited her to dance the part of Laurey in the show's famous dream sequence. The role had been ideal for a budding young ballerina, and Kat had loved her first true chance to perform. There had been costumes and makeup and lights—and there had been Rye Harmon.

Rye had been the star pitcher on the high school baseball team, with a reasonable baritone voice and an easy manner that translated well to the high school auditorium stage. Sure, he didn't know the first thing about dancing, but with careful choreography, the audience never discovered the truth. Week after week, Kat had nurtured a silly crush on her partner, even though she *knew* it could never amount to anything. Not when she was a precocious middle-school brat, and he was a high school hero. Not when she had her entire New York career ahead of herself, and he was Eden Falls incarnate—born, bred and content to stay in town forever.

In the intervening years, Kat had danced on stages around the world. She had kissed and been kissed a thousand times—in ballets and in real life, too. She was a grown, competent, mature woman, come back to town to help her family when they needed her most.

But she was also the child who had lived in Eden Falls, the shy girl who had craved attention from the unattainable senior.

And so she reacted the way a classically trained New York ballerina would act. She raised her chin. She narrowed her eyes. She tilted her head slightly to the right. And she said, "I'm sorry. Have we met?"

Rye stopped short as Kat Morehouse pinned him with her silver-gray eyes. He had no doubt that he was looking at Kat and not her twin, Rachel. Kat had always been the sister with the cool reserve, with the poised pride, even before she'd left Eden Falls. When was that? Ten years ago? Rye had just graduated from high school, but he'd still been impressed with all the gossip about one of Eden Falls's own heading up to New York City to make her fortune at some fancy ballet school.

Of course, Rye had seen plenty of Kat's sister, Rachel, around town over the past decade. Done more than see her, six years ago. He'd actually dated her for three of the most tempestuous weeks of his life. She'd been six months out of high school then, and she had flirted with him mercilessly, showing up at job sites, throwing pebbles at his window until he came down to see her in the middle of the night. It had taken him a while to figure out that she was just bent on getting revenge against one of Rye's fraternity brothers, Josh Barton. Barton had dumped her, saying she was nuts.

It had taken Rye just a few weeks to reach the same conclusion, then a few more to extricate himself from Rachel's crazy, melodramatic life. Just as well—a couple of months later, Rachel had turned up pregnant. Rye could still remember the frozen wave of disbelief that had washed over him when she told him the news, the shattering sound of all his dreams crashing to earth. And he could still remember stammering out a promise to be there for Rachel, to support his child. Most of all, though, he recalled the searing rush of relief when Rachel laughed, told him the baby was Josh's, entitled to its own share of the legendary Barton fortune.

Rye had dodged a bullet there.

If he had fathered Rachel's daughter—what was her name? Jessica? Jennifer?—he never could have left town. Never could have moved up to Richmond, set up his own contracting business. As it was, it had taken him six years after that wake-up call, and he still felt the constant demands of his family, had felt it with half a dozen girlfriends over the years. With a kid in the picture, he never could have fulfilled his vow to be a fully independent contractor by his thirtieth birthday.

He'd been well shed of Rachel, six years ago.

And he had no doubt he was looking at Kat now. Rachel and Kat were about as opposite as any two human beings could be—even if they were sisters. Even if they were twins. Kat's sharp eyes were the same as they'd been in middle school—but that was the only resemblance she bore to the freakishly good dancer he had once known.

That Kat Morehouse had been a kid.

This Kat Morehouse was a woman.

She was a full head taller than when he'd seen her last. Skinnier, too, all long legs and bare arms and a neck that looked like it was carved out of rare marble. Her jet-black hair was piled on top of her head in some sort of spiky ponytail, but he could see that it would be long and straight and thick, if she ever let it down. She was wearing a trim black T-shirt and matching jeans that looked like they'd been specially sewn in Paris or Italy or one of those fashion places.

And she had a bright blue walking boot on her left leg—the sort of boot that he'd worn through a few injuries over the years. The sort of boot that itched like hell in the heat. The sort of boot that made it a pain to stand on the edge of a ragged blacktop parking lot in front of the Eden Falls train station, waiting for a ride that was obviously late or, more likely, not coming at all.

Rye realized he was still standing there, his hand extended toward Kat like he was some idiot farm boy gawking at the state fair Dairy Princess. He squared his shoulders and wiped his palms across the worn denim thighs of his jeans. From the ice in Kat's platinum gaze, she clearly had no recollection of who he was. Well, at least he could fix that.

He stepped forward, finally closing the distance between them. "Rye," he said by way of introduction. "Rye Harmon. We met in high school. I mean, when I was in high school. You were in middle school. I was Curly, in *Oklahoma.* I mean, the play."

Yeah, genius, Rye thought to himself. *Like she really thought you meant Oklahoma, the state.*

Kat hadn't graduated from the National Ballet School without plenty of acting classes. She put those skills to good use, flashing a bright smile of supposedly sudden recognition. "Rye!" she said. "Of course!"

She sounded fake to herself, but she suspected no one else could tell. Well, maybe her mother. Her father. Rachel, if she bothered to pay attention. But certainly not a practical stranger like Rye Harmon. A practical stranger who said, "Going to your folks' house? I can drop you there." He reached for her overnight bag, as if his assistance was a forgone conclusion.

"Oh, no," she protested. "I couldn't ask you to do that!" She grabbed for the handle of the roller bag as well, flinching when her fingers settled on top of his. What was *wrong* with her? She wasn't usually this jumpy.

She wasn't usually in Eden Falls, Virginia.

"It's no problem," Rye said, and she remembered that easy smile from a decade before. "Your parents live three blocks from mine—from where I'm taking Lisa."

Kat wanted to say no. She had been solving her own problems for ten long years.

Not that she had such a great track record lately. Her walking boot was testament to that. And the box of things piled in the corner of her bedroom, waiting for cheating Adam to pick up while she was out of town.

But what was she going to do? Watch Rye drive out of the parking lot, and then discover she had no change at the bottom of her purse? Or that the pay phone—if there even *was* a pay phone—was out of order? Or that no one was at the Morehouse home, that Mike had some doctor's appointment Susan had forgotten when they made their plans?

"Okay," Kat said, only then realizing that her hand was still on Rye's, that they both still held her suitcase. "Um, thanks."

She let him take the bag, hobbling after him to the gleaming truck. Lisa shifted over on the bench seat, saying, "Hey," in a friendly voice.

"Hi," Kat answered, aware of the Northern inflection in her voice, of the clipped vowel sound that made her seem like she was in a hurry. She *was* in a hurry, though. She'd come all the way from New York City— almost five hundred miles.

It wasn't just the distance, though. It was the lifetime. It was the return to her awkward, unhappy childhood, where she'd always been the odd one out, the dancer, the kid who was destined to move away.

She'd left Eden Falls for a reason—to build her dream career. Now that she was back in the South, she felt like her life was seizing up in quicksand. She was being forced to move slower, trapped by convention and expectation and the life she had not led.

Determined to regain a bit of control, she turned back to the truck door, ready to tug it closed behind her. She was startled to find Rye standing there. "Oh!" she said, leaping away. The motion tumbled her purse from her lap to her feet. Silently cursing her uncharacteristic lack of grace, she leaned forward to scoop everything back inside her bag. Rye reached out to help, but she angled her shoulder, finishing the embarrassing task before he could join in.

"I didn't mean to startle you," he drawled. He reached inside the truck and passed her the seat belt, pulling it forward from its awkward position over her right shoulder.

"You didn't!" But, of course, he had. And if she made any more protest, he might take more time to apologize, time she did not want to waste. It was all well and good for him to take all day on a run to the train station. What else could he have to do in slow-paced Eden Falls? But she was there to help her family, and she might as well get started. She pulled the seat belt across her chest, settling it in its slot with the precision of a brain surgeon. "I'm fine. And if you don't mind, I'm sort of in a hurry."

She almost winced when she realized how brusque she sounded.

Recognizing dismissal when he heard it, Rye shut the door carefully. He shook his head as he walked around the front of his truck. Ten years had passed, but he still remembered Kat's precise attention to detail. Kat Morehouse had been a determined girl. And she had clearly grown into a formidable woman.

Formidable. Not exactly the type he was used to dating. Certainly not like Rachel had been, with her constant breaking of rules, pushing of boundaries. And not like the sweet, small-town girls he had dated here in Eden Falls.

His brothers teased him, saying he'd moved to Richmond because he needed a deeper dating pool. Needed to find a real woman—all the girls in Eden Falls knew him too well.

He hadn't actually had time for a date in the past year—not since he'd been burned by Marissa. Marissa Turner. He swallowed the bitter taste in his mouth as he thought of the woman who had been his girlfriend for two long years. Two long years, when he had torn apart his own life plans, forfeited his fledgling business, all to support her beauty salon.

Every time Rye mentioned making it big in Richmond, Marissa had thrown a fit. He had wanted her to be happy, and so he had circumscribed all of his dreams. It was easier, after all. Easier to stay in Eden Falls. Easier to keep doing the same handyman work he'd been doing all of his adult life. At least Marissa was happy.

Until she got some crazy-ass chance to work on a movie out in Hollywood, doing the hair for some leading-man hunk. Marissa had flown cross-country without a single look back, not even bothering to break up with Rye by phone. And he had been left utterly alone, feeling like a fool.

A fool who was two years behind on his business plan.

But not anymore. With Marissa gone, Rye had finally made the leap, moving up to Richmond, finding the perfect office, hunting down a tolerable apartment. He was finally moving on with his life, and it felt damn good to make choices for himself. Not for his family. Not for his girlfriend. For him.

At least, most of the time.

Lisa was chatting with Kat by the time he settled into the driver's seat. "It's no problem, really," his sister was saying. "Rye already came down from Richmond to get me. Things are crazy at home—Mama's out West visiting her sister, and Daddy's busy with the spring planting. Half my brothers and sisters sent up a distress call to get Rye home for the weekend. He's walking dogs for our sister Jordana—she's out of town for a wedding, so she can't take care of her usual clients. At least he could fit taxi service in before coaching T-ball practice this afternoon, filling in for Noah."

Listening to Lisa's friendly banter, Rye had to shake his head. It was no wonder he had moved all the way to Richmond to make his business work. Of course, he loved his family, loved the fact that they all looked to him to fix whatever was wrong. But here in Eden Falls, there was *always* a brother who needed a hand, a sister with one more errand, cousins, aunts, uncles, friends— *people* who pulled him away from his business.

He'd only been living in Richmond for a month, and he'd already come back to Eden Falls a half-dozen times. He promised himself he'd get more control over his calendar in the weeks to come.

Lisa nudged his ribs with a sharp elbow. "Right? Tell Kat that it's no big deal, or she's going to get out at the traffic light and walk home from there!"

Rye couldn't help but smile. He could grouse all he wanted about being called home, but he loved his family, loved the fact that they needed him. "It's no big deal," he said dutifully, and then he nodded to Kat. "And you shouldn't be walking anywhere on that boot. Broken foot?"

Kat fought against her automatic frown. "Stress fracture."

"Ow. Our brother Logan had one of those, a couple of years back. He plays baseball for the Eagles. It took about a month for his foot to heal. A month until he could get back to playing, anyway."

Kat started to ask if Logan pitched, like Rye had done, but then she remembered she wasn't supposed to have recognized Rye. She settled for shrugging instead and saying, "The doctors say I've got about a month to wait, myself. I figured it was a good time to come down here. Help out my parents."

Rye gave her a sympathetic glance. "I was at their house a few months ago, to install a handheld shower for your father. How's he doing?"

"Fine." Kat curved her lips into the smile she had mastered in her long-ago acting classes. Her father was fine. Susan was fine. Jenny was fine. Everyone was fine, and Kat would be on a northbound train in less than a week.

"Colon cancer can be rough." Rye's voice was filled with sympathy.

"They say they caught it in time." Kat was afraid to voice her fears—Mike's recovery had taken longer than anyone had expected. He'd been in and out of the hospital for six months, and now, with pneumonia...

At least Rye seemed to believe her. He didn't ask any more questions. Instead, he assured her, "Everyone's been real worried about them. Just last week, my mother had me bring by some of her chicken almond casserole. It'll get your father back on his feet in no time."

Kat couldn't remember the last time she'd cooked for a sick friend. Oh, well. Things were different down here. People had different ways to show they cared. She tried to recall the lessons in politeness that her mother had drilled into her, years before. "I'm sure it was delicious. It was kind of you to bring it by."

Rye wondered if he'd somehow made Kat angry—she sounded so stiff. Her hands were folded in her lap, her fingers wrapped around each other in perfect precision, like coils of rope, fresh from the factory. She sat upright like a soldier, keeping her spine from touching the back of her seat. Her eyes flashed as they drove past familiar streets, and each intersection tightened the cords in her throat.

And then it came to him: Kat wasn't angry. She was frightened.

One thing Rye had learned in almost thirty years of dealing with siblings and cousins was how to ease the mind of someone who was afraid. Just talk to them. It was easy enough to spin out a story or two about Eden Falls. He might have moved away, but he could always dredge up something entertaining about the only real home he'd ever known.

He nodded to the row of little shops they were passing. "Miss Emily just closed up her pet store."

Kat barely glanced at the brightly painted storefront, and for a second he thought she might not take the bait. Finally, though, she asked, "What happened?"

"She couldn't stand to see any of the animals in cages. She sold off all the mice and gerbils and fish, and then she took in a couple of litters of kittens. She gave them free rein over the whole shop. Problem was, she fell in love with the kittens too much to sell them. If she took money, she couldn't be sure the animals were going to a good home. So instead of selling them, she gave them away to the best owners she could find. In the end, she decided it didn't make much sense to pay rent. Anyone who wants a kitten now just goes up to her house and knocks on the front door."

There. That was better. He actually caught a hint of a smile on Kat's lips. Lisa, of course, was rolling her eyes, but at least his sister didn't call him a liar. As long as he was on a roll, he nodded toward the elementary school they were passing. "Remember classes there? They had to skip the Christmas pageant last December because the boa constrictor in the fourth-grade classroom got out. None of the parents would come see the show until the snake was found. The kids are going to sing 'Jingle Bells' for the Easter parade."

Kat couldn't help herself. She had to ask. "Did they ever find the snake?"

"He finally came out about a week ago. The janitor found him sunning himself on the parking lot, none the worse for wear. He was hungry, though. They used to feed him mice from Miss Emily's."

Kat wrinkled her nose, but she had to laugh. She had to admit—she couldn't imagine the National Ballet School having similar problems. And they would *never* have postponed a performance, snake or no snake, especially a holiday showcase like a Christmas pageant.

Rye eased up to the curb in front of her parents' house, shoving the gearshift into Park. He hopped out of the truck as Kat said goodbye to Lisa. She joined him by the deep bed. "Thank you," she said. And somehow, she meant to thank him for more than the ride. She meant to tell him that she appreciated the effort he had made, the way that he had tried to distract her from her worry.

"My pleasure," he said, tipping an imaginary hat. "Harmon Contracting is a full-service provider." He hefted her suitcase out of the truck, shrugging it into a more comfortable position as he nodded for Kat to precede him up the driveway.

"Oh, I can get that," she said, reaching for the bag.

"It's no problem."

"Please," she said, carving an edge onto the word. She'd learned long ago how to get her way in the bustling streets of New York. She knew the precise angle to hold her shoulders, the exact line to set her chin. No one would dare argue with her when she'd strapped on her big city armor.

Rye recognized that stance; he'd seen it often enough in his own sisters, in his mother. Kat Morehouse was not going to give in easily.

And there really wasn't any reason to push the matter. It wasn't as if he didn't have a thousand other things to do that afternoon—the dog walking Lisa had mentioned, and the T-ball practice, but also phone calls back to Richmond, trying to keep his fledgling business alive while he was on the road.

And yet, he really didn't want to leave Kat here, alone. If he turned his head just a little, he could still see the girl she'd been, the stubborn, studious child who had defied convention, who had done what *she* wanted to do, had carved out the life *she* wanted, never letting little Eden Falls stop her in her tracks.

But there would be time enough to see Kat again. She wasn't going to disappear overnight, and he was in town for the whole weekend. He could stop by the next day. Think of some excuse between now and then. He extended the handle on the roller bag, turning it around to make it easier for Kat to grasp. "Have it your way," he said, adding a smile.

"Thanks," Kat said, and she hustled up the driveway, relying on the roller bag to disguise the lurch of her booted foot. Only when she reached the door did she wonder if she should go back to Rye's truck, thank him properly for the ride. After all, he'd done her a real favor, bringing her home. And she wouldn't mind taking one last look at those slate-black eyes, at the smooth planes of his face, at his rugged jaw....

She shook her head, though, reminding herself to concentrate. She was through with men. Through with distractions that just consumed her time, that took her away from the things that were truly important, from the things that mattered. She might have been an idiot to get involved with Adam, but at least she could translate her disappointing experience into something useful.

Waving a calculatedly jaunty farewell toward Rye and Lisa, Kat threw back her shoulders, took a deep breath and turned the doorknob. Of course the front door was unlocked; it always was. In New York, Kat had to work three different locks on the door of the apartment she shared with Haley, every single time she went in or out. Things were simpler here in Eden Falls. Easier. Safer.

Boring.

Pushing down her automatic derogatory thoughts about the town that had kept her parents happy for their entire lives, Kat stepped over the threshold. And then she caught her breath at the scene inside the old brick rambler.

Chaos. Utter, complete chaos.

A radio blasted from the kitchen, some mournful weatherman announcing that the temperature was going to top ninety, a new record high for the last day in March. A teakettle shrieked on the stovetop, piercing the entire house with its urgent demand. In the living room, a television roared the jingle from a video game, the same four bars of music, over and over and over again. From the master bedroom, a man shouted, "Fine! Let me do it, then!" and a shrill child's voice repeated, "I'm helping! I'm helping!"

All of a sudden, it seemed pretty clear how Susan had forgotten to meet Kat at the train station.

Resisting the urge to hobble back to the curb and

beg Rye to take her to a motel out on the highway—or better yet, back to the train station so she could catch the two-fifteen northbound Clipper—Kat closed the front door behind her. She pushed her little suitcase into the corner of the foyer and dropped her purse beside it. She headed to the kitchen first, grabbing a pot holder from the side of the refrigerator where her mother had kept them forever. The kettle stopped screaming as soon as she lifted it from the heat. The blue flame died immediately when Kat turned the knob on the stove. She palmed off the radio before the local news break could end.

Next stop was the living room, where Kat cast the television into silence, resorting to pushing buttons on the actual set, rather than seeking out the missing remote control. A scramble of half-clothed Barbie dolls lay on the floor, pink dresses tangled with a rose-colored sports car that had plunged into a dry fuchsia swimming pool. A handful of board games was splattered across the entire mess—tiny cones from Sorry mixing with Jenga rods and piles of Monopoly money. Kat shook her head—there would be plenty of time to sort that mess later.

And that left the voices coming from the master bedroom, down the hallway. Kat could make out her father's gruff tones as he insisted someone hand him something immediately. The whining child—it had to be Jenny—was still saying "I'm helping," as if she had to prove her worthiness to someone. And Kat surprised herself by finding tears in her eyes when she heard a low murmur—her calm, unflappable mother, trying to soothe both her husband and her granddaughter.

Kat clumped down the hall, resenting the awkward

walking boot more than ever. When she reached the doorway, she was surprised by the tableau before her.

A hospital bed loomed between her parents' ancient double mattress and the far wall. Mike lay prone between the raised bars, but he craned his neck at a sharp angle. He held out a calloused hand, demanding that a tiny raven-haired child hand over the controls to the bed. The girl kept pressing buttons without any effect; she obviously did not understand how to make the bed work. Susan was framed in the doorway to the bathroom, her gray face cut deep with worry lines as she balanced a small tray, complete with a glass of water and a cup of pills.

"Kat!" Susan exclaimed. "What time—?"

"I caught a ride home with Rye Harmon," Kat said, wrestling to keep her gait as close to normal as possible. The last thing she wanted was for her mother to fuss over a stupid stress fracture. Not when Susan obviously had so much else to worry about.

Kat plucked the bed controls from her niece's hand and passed the bulky plastic block to her father. She settled firm fingers on the child's shoulder, turning her toward the doorway and the living room. "Thank you, Jenny," she said, pushing pretend warmth into the words. "You were a big help. Now there are some toys out there, just waiting for you to straighten up."

Jenny sighed, but she shuffled down the hallway. Kat leaned down to brush a kiss against her father's forehead, easing an arm beneath his shoulders as he started to manipulate the mechanical bed, fighting to raise himself into a seated position. When she was certain he was more comfortable, Kat said, "Come sit down, Mama." She heard the hard New York edge on her words, and she smiled to soften her voice. "Why don't you rest, and let me take care of that for a while?"

Even as Susan settled on the edge of the double bed, Kat heard the distant whistle of the Clipper, the New York-bound train, leaving town for the day. The wild, lonesome sound immediately made her think about Rye Harmon, about how he had offered to come inside, to help. He'd scooped her up from the train station like a knight in shining armor—a friendly, easygoing knight whom she'd known all her life. Kat blinked and she could see his kind smile, his warm black eyes. She could picture the steady, sturdy way he had settled her into his truck.

She shook her head. She didn't have time to think about Rye. Instead, she handed her father his medicine, taking care to balance her weight, keeping her spine in alignment despite her cursed walking boot. She had come to Eden Falls to help out her family, to be there for Susan and Mike. And as soon as humanly possible, she was heading back to New York, and the National Ballet Company and the life she had worked so hard to attain. She didn't have time for Rye Harmon. Rye Harmon, or anything else that might delay her escape from Eden Falls.

Chapter Two

Three hours later, Kat wondered if she had made the greatest mistake of her life. She leaned against the headrest in her cousin Amanda's ancient sedan, resisting the urge to strangle her five-year-old niece.

"But *why* isn't Aunt Kat driving?" Jenny asked for the fourth time.

"I'm happy to drive you both home, Jenny," Amanda deflected, applying one of the tricks she'd learned as a schoolteacher.

"But *why*—"

Kat interrupted the whining question, spitting out an answer through gritted teeth. "Because I don't know how!"

Amanda laughed at Kat's frustration. The cousins had been quite close when they were children—certainly closer than Kat had been to her own sister. Nevertheless, Amanda always thought it was hysterical that

Kat had never gotten her driver's license. More than once, she had teased Kat about moving away to the magical kingdom of Oz, where she was carried around by flying monkeys.

Jenny, though, wasn't teasing Kat. The five-year-old child was simply astonished, her mouth stretched into an amazed O before she stammered, "B-but *all* grown-ups know how to drive!"

"Maybe your Aunt Kat isn't a grown-up," Amanda suggested helpfully.

Kat gave her a dirty look before saying, "I am a grown-up, Jenny, but I don't drive. The two things are totally separate."

"But how do you go to the grocery store?"

"I walk there," Kat said, exasperated. How could one little girl make her feel like such a sideshow freak?

"But what do you do with the bags of groceries?"

"I carry them!"

Kat's voice was rough enough that even the headstrong Jenny declined to ask another follow-up question. It wasn't so ridiculous, that Kat couldn't drive. She'd left Eden Falls when she was fourteen, long before she'd even thought of getting behind the wheel of a car. She'd spent the next ten years living in Manhattan, where subways, buses and the occasional taxi met her transportation needs. Anything heavy or bulky could be delivered.

But try explaining that to someone who had never even heard of the Mason-Dixon line, much less traveled above it.

Amanda's laugh smoothed over the awkward moment as she pulled into the driveway of a run-down brick Colonial. Weeds poked through the crumbling asphalt, and the lawn was long dead from lack of water—

just as well, since it had not been cut for months. One shutter hung at a defeated angle, and the screen on the front door was slashed and rusted. A collapsing carport signaled imminent danger to any vehicle unfortunate enough to be parked beneath it.

"I don't believe it!" Kat said. The last time she had seen this house, it had been neat and trim, kept in perfect shape. Years ago, it had belonged to her grandmother, to Susan's mother. The Morehouses had kept it in the family after Granny died; it was easy enough to keep up the little Colonial.

Easy enough, that was, until Rachel got her hands on the place. Susan and Mike had let Rachel move in after she'd graduated from high school, when the constant fights had become too difficult under their own roof. The arrangement had been intended to be temporary, but once Rachel gave birth to Jenny, it had somehow slipped into something permanent.

Now, though, looking at the wreck of Granny's neat little home, Kat could not help but begrudge that decision. Did Rachel destroy *everything* she touched?

Amanda's voice shone with forced brightness. "It always looks bad after winter. Once everything's freshened up for spring, it'll be better."

Sure it would. Because Rachel had such a green thumb, she had surely taken care of basic gardening over the past several years. Rachel always worked so hard to bring good things into her life. Not.

Kat swallowed hard and undid her seat belt. *One week,* she reminded herself. She only had to stay here one week. Then Jenny could return to Susan and Mike. Or, who knew? Rachel might even be back from wherever she had gone. "Well…" Kat tried to think of something positive to say about the house. Failing miserably, she fell back on something she *could* be grateful for. "Thanks for the ride."

Amanda's soft features settled into a frown. "Do you need any help with your bag? Are you sure—"

"We'll be fine."

"We could all go out to dinner—"

That was the last thing Kat wanted—drawing out the day, eating in some Eden Falls greasy spoon, where the food would send any thinking dancer to the workout room for at least ten straight hours, just to break even. Besides, she really didn't want to impose on her cousin's good nature—and driver's license—any more than was strictly necessary. "We'll be *fine,* Amanda. I'm sure Aunt Sarah and Uncle Bill are already wondering what took you so long, just running Jenny and me across town. You don't want them to start worrying."

At least Kat's case was bolstered by her niece's behavior. Jenny had already hopped out of her seat and scuffed her way to the faded front door. Amanda sighed. "I don't know what sort of food you'll find in there, Kat."

"We can always—" What? She was going to say, they could always have D'Agostino deliver groceries. But there wasn't a D'Agostino in Eden Falls. There wasn't *any* grocery store that delivered. She swallowed hard and pushed her way through to the end of the sentence. "We can always order a pizza."

That was the right thing to say. Amanda relaxed, obviously eased by the sheer normalcy of Kat's suggestion.

As *if* Kat would eat a pizza. She'd given up mozzarella the year she'd first gone on pointe. "Thanks so much for the ride," Kat said. "Give my love to Aunt Sarah and Uncle Bill."

By the time Kat dragged her roller bag through the front door, Jenny was in the kitchen, kneeling on a chair in front of the open pantry. Her hand was shoved deep in a bag of cookies, and telltale chocolate crumbs ringed her lips. Kat's reproach was automatic. "Are you eating cookies for dinner?"

"No." Jenny eyed her defiantly.

"Don't lie to me, young lady." *Ach*, Kat thought. *Did I really just say that? I sound like everyone's stereotype of the strict maiden aunt.* Annoyed, Kat looked around the kitchen. Used paper plates cascaded out of an open trash can. A jar of peanut butter lay on its side, its lid teetering at a crazy angle. A dozen plastic cups were strewn across the counter, with varying amounts of sticky residue pooling inside.

On top of the toaster oven curled three bananas. Kat broke one off from the bunch and passed it to her niece. "Here", she said. "Eat this."

"I don't like them when they're brown."

"That's dinner."

"You said we were ordering a pizza."

"Pizza isn't good for you."

"Mommy likes pizza."

"Mommy would." Kat closed her eyes and took a deep breath. This wasn't the time or the place to get into a discussion about Rachel. Kat dug in the pantry, managing to excavate a sealed packet of lemon-pepper tuna. "Here. You can have tuna and a banana. I'll go to the grocery store tomorrow."

"How are you going to do that, when you don't drive? It's too far to walk."

Good question. "I'll manage."

Kat took a quick tour of the rest of the house while Jenny ate her dinner. Alas, the kitchen wasn't some terrible aberration. The living room was ankle-deep in pizza boxes and gossip magazines. The disgusting bathroom hadn't been cleaned in centuries. Jenny's bedroom was a sea of musty, tangled sheets and stuffed animals.

Back in the kitchen, Jenny's sullen silence was nearly enough to make Kat put cookies back on the menu. Almost. But Jenny didn't need cookies. She needed some rules. Some structure. A pattern or two in her life. Starting now.

"Okay, kiddo. We're going to get some cleaning done."

"Cleaning?" Jenny's whine stretched the word into four or five syllables at least.

Kat turned to the stove—ironically, the cleanest thing in the house, because Rachel had never cooked a meal in her life. Kat twisted the old-fashioned timer to give them fifteen minutes to work. "Let's go. Fifteen minutes, to make this kitchen look new."

Jenny stared at her as if she'd lost her mind. Squaring her shoulders, though, and ignoring the blooming ache in her foot, Kat started to tame the pile of paper plates. "Let's go," she said. "March! You're in charge of throwing away those paper cups!"

With the use of three supersize trash bags, they made surprising progress. When those fifteen minutes were done, Kat set the alarm again, targeting the mess in the living room. The bathroom was next, and finally Jenny's room. The little girl was yawning and rubbing her eyes by the time they finished.

"Mommy never makes me clean up."

"I'm not Mommy," Kat said. She was *so* not Mommy—not in a million different ways. But she knew what was good for Jenny. She knew what had been good for her, even when she was Jenny's age. Setting goals. Developing strategies. Following rules. When Kat had lived in her parents' home, Susan had built the foundation for orderly management of life's problems. Unlike her sister, Kat had absorbed those lessons with a vengeance. Her *rules* were the only thing that had gotten her through those first homesick months when she moved to New York. As Jenny started to collapse on the living-room couch, Kat said, "It's time for you to go to bed."

"I haven't watched TV yet!"

"No TV. It's a school night."

"Mommy lets me watch TV every night."

"I'm not Mommy," Kat repeated, wondering if she should record the sentence, so that she could play it back every time she needed it.

Over the next half hour, Kat found out that she was cruel and heartless and evil and mean, just like the worst villains of Jenny's favorite animated movies. But the child eventually got to bed wearing her pajamas, with her teeth brushed, her hair braided and her prayers said.

Exhausted, and unwilling to admit just how much her foot was aching, Kat collapsed onto the sagging living-room couch. Six more days. She could take six more days of anything. They couldn't all be this difficult. She glanced at her watch and was shocked to see it was only eight-thirty.

That left her plenty of time to call Haley. Plenty of time to catch up on the exploits of Adam and Selene, to remember why Kat was so much better off without that miserable excuse for a man in her life.

Kat summoned her willpower and stumped over to her purse, where she'd left it on the kitchen table.

She rooted for her cell phone. Nothing. She scrambled around, digging past her wallet. Still nothing. She dumped the contents out on the kitchen table, where it immediately became clear that she had no cell phone.

And then she remembered spilling everything in the cab of Rye's truck in her rush of surprise to see him standing beside her. She had been shocked by the elemental response to his body near hers. She'd acted like a silly schoolgirl, like a brainless child, jumping the way she had, dropping her purse.

But even as she berated herself, she remembered Rye's easy smile. He'd been truly gallant, rescuing her at the train station. It had been mean of her to pretend not to remember him. Uncomfortably, she thought of the confused flash in his eyes, the tiny flicker of hurt that was almost immediately smothered beneath the blanket of his good nature.

And then, her belly did that funny thing again, that flutter that was part nervous anticipation, part unreasoning dread. The closest thing she could compare it to was the thrill of opening night, the excitement of standing in the wings while a new audience hummed in the theater's red-velvet seats.

But she wasn't in the theater. She was in Eden Falls.

And whether she wanted to or not, Kat was going to have to track down Rye Harmon the following day. Track him down, and retrieve her phone, and hope she had a better signal at Rachel's house than she'd had at the station.

All things considered, though, she couldn't get too upset about the lack of signal that she'd encountered. If she'd been able to call Susan or Amanda, then Rye would never have given her a ride. And those few minutes of talking with Rye Harmon had been the high point of her very long, very stressful, very exhausting first afternoon and evening in Eden Falls.

By noon the next day, Kat had decided that retrieving her cell phone was the least of her concerns.

Susan had swung by that morning, just after Kat had hustled a reluctant Jenny onto her school bus. Looking around the straightened house, Susan said, "It looks like you and Jenny were busy last night."

"The place was a pigsty."

"I'm sorry, dear. I just wasn't able to get over here before you arrived, to clean things up."

Kat immediately felt terrible for her judgmental tone. "I wasn't criticizing *you,* Mama. I just can't believe Rachel lives like that."

Susan shook her head. Kat knew from long experience that her mother would never say anything directly critical about her other daughter. But sometimes Susan's silences echoed with a thousand shades of meaning.

Pushing aside a lifetime of criticism about her sister, Kat said, "Thank you so much for bringing by that casserole. Jenny and I will really enjoy it tonight."

Susan apologized again. "I can't believe I didn't think of giving you anything last night. The church ladies have been so helpful—they've kept our freezer stocked for months."

"I'm glad you've had that type of support," Kat said. And she was. She still couldn't imagine any of her friends in New York cooking for a colleague in need. Certainly no one would organize food week after week. "How was Daddy last night? Did either of you get any sleep?"

Susan's smile was brilliant, warming Kat from

across the room. "Oh, yes, sweetheart. I had to wake him up once for his meds, but he fell back to sleep right away. It was the best night he's had in months."

Glancing around the living room, Kat swallowed a proud grin. She had been right to come down here. If one night could help Susan so much, what would an entire week accomplish?

Susan went on. "And it was a godsend, not fixing breakfast for Jenny before the sun was up. That elementary school bus comes so early, it's a crime."

Kat was accustomed to being awake well before the sun rose. She usually fit in ninety minutes on the treadmill in the company gym before she even thought about attending her first dance rehearsal of the day. Of course, with the walking boot, she hadn't been able to indulge in the tension tamer of her typical exercise routine. She'd had to make due with a punishing regimen of crunches instead, alternating sets with modified planks and a series of leg lifts meant to keep her hamstrings as close to dancing strength as possible.

As for Jenny's breakfast? It had been some hideous purple-and-green cereal, eaten dry, because there wasn't any milk in the house. Kat had been willing to concede the point on cold cereal first thing in the morning, but she had silently vowed that the artificially dyed stuff would be out of the house by the time Jenny got home that afternoon. Whole-grain oats would be better for the little girl—and they wouldn't stain the milk in Jenny's bowl.

There'd be time enough to pick up some groceries that afternoon. For now, Kat knew her mother had another task in mind. "So, are you going to drop me off at the studio now?"

Susan looked worried. "It's really too much for me

to ask. I shouldn't even have mentioned it when I called you, dear. I'm sure I can take care of everything in the next couple of weeks."

"Don't be silly," Kat said. "I know Rachel was running things for you. She's been gone for a while, though, and someone has to pick up the slack. I came to Eden Falls to help."

Susan fussed some more, but she was already leading the way out to her car. It may have been ten years since Kat had lived in Eden Falls, but she knew the way to the Morehouse Dance Academy by heart. As a child, she had practically lived in her mother's dance studio, from the moment she could pull on her first leotard.

The building was smaller than she remembered, though. It seemed lost in the sea of its huge parking lot. A broken window was covered over with a cardboard box, and a handful of yellowed newspapers rested against the door, like kindling.

Kat glanced at her mother's pinched face, and she consciously coated her next words with a smile. "Don't worry, Mama. It'll just take a couple of hours to make sure everything is running smoothly. Go home and take care of Daddy. I'll call Amanda to bring me back to Rachel's."

"Let me just come in with you...."

Kat shook her head. Once her mother started in on straightening the studio, she'd stay all morning. Susan wasn't the sort of woman to walk away from a project half-done. Even *if* she had a recuperating husband who needed her back at the house.

"I'll be fine, Mama. I know this place like the back of my hand. And I'm sure Rachel left everything in good shape."

Good shape. Right.

The roof was leaking in the main classroom, a slow drip that had curled up the ceiling tiles and stained one wall. Kat shuddered to think about the state of the warped hardwood floor. Both toilets were running in the public restroom, and the sinks were stained from dripping faucets. Kat ran the hot water for five minutes before she gave up on getting more than an icy trickle.

The damage wasn't limited to the building. When Kat turned on the main computer, she heard a grinding sound, and the screen flashed blue before it died altogether. The telephone handset was sticky; a quick sniff confirmed that someone had handled it with maple syrup on their fingers.

In short, the dance studio was an absolute and complete mess.

Kat seethed. How could students be taking classes here? How could her parents' hard-earned investment be ruined so quickly? What had Rachel done?

Muttering to herself, Kat started to sift through the papers on the desk in the small, paneled office. She found a printout of an electronic spreadsheet—at least the computer had been functional back in January.

The news on the spreadsheet, though, told a depressing story. Class sizes for the winter term had dwindled from their robust fall enrollment. Many of those payments had never been collected. Digging deeper, Kat found worse news—a dozen checks, dating back to September—had never been cashed. Search as she might, she could find no checks at all for the spring term; she couldn't even find an enrollment list for the classes.

Susan had been absolutely clear, every time Kat talked to her: Rachel had shaped up. Rachel had run the dance studio for the past six months, ever since

Mike's diagnosis had thrown Susan's life into utter disarray. Rachel had lined up teachers, had taken care of the books, had kept everything functioning like clockwork.

Rachel had lied through her teeth.

Kat's fingers trembled with rage as she looked around the studio. Her heart pounded, and her breath came in short gasps. Tears pricked at the corners of her eyes, angry tears that made her chew on her lower lip.

And so Kat did the only thing she knew how to do. She tried to relieve her stress the only way she could. She walked across the floor of the classroom, her feet automatically turning out in a ballerina's stance, even though she wore her hated blue boot. Resenting that handicap, she planted her good foot, setting one hand on the barre with a lifetime of familiarity.

She closed her eyes and ran through the simplest of exercises. First position, second position, third position, fourth. She swept her free arm in a graceful arc, automatically tilting her head to an angle that maximized the long line of her neck. She repeated the motions again, three times, four. Each pass through, she felt a little of her tension drain, a little of her rage fade.

She was almost able to take a lung-filling breath when heavy footsteps dragged her back to messy, disorganized reality. "*There* you are!"

Rye stopped in the doorway, frozen into place by the vision of Kat at the barre. All of a sudden, he was catapulted back ten years in time, to the high school auditorium, to the rough stage where he had plodded through the role of Curly.

He had caught Kat stretching out for dancing there, too, backstage one spring afternoon. She'd had her heel firmly anchored on a table, bending her willowy limbs with a grace that had made his own hulking, teenage body awaken to desire. He could see her now, only a few feet away, close enough for him to touch.

But his interest had been instantly quenched when he'd glimpsed Kat's face, that day so long ago. Tears had tracked down her smooth cheeks, silvering the rosy skin that was completely bare of the blush and concealer and all the other makeup crap that high school girls used. Even as he took one step closer, he had seen her flinch, caught her eyes darting toward the dressing room. He'd heard the brassy laugh of one of the senior girls, one of the cheerleaders, and he'd immediately understood that the popular kids had been teasing the young middle-school dancer. Again.

Rye had done the only thing that made sense at the time, the one thing that he thought would make Kat forget that she was an outsider. He'd leaned forward to brush a quick fraternal kiss against her cheek.

But somehow—even now, he couldn't say how—he'd ended up touching his lips to hers. They'd been joined for just a heartbeat, a single, chaste connection that had jolted through him with the power of a thousand sunsets.

Rye could still remember the awkward blush that had flamed his face. He really had meant to kiss her on the cheek. He'd swear it—on his letter jacket and his game baseball, and everything else that had mattered to him back in high school. He had no idea if he had moved wrong, or if she had, but after the kiss she had leaped away as if he'd scorched her with a blowtorch.

Thinking back, Rye still wanted to wince. How had he screwed *that* up? He had three sisters. He had a lifetime of experience kissing cheeks, offering old-fashioned, brotherly support. He'd certainly never kissed one of his sisters on the lips by mistake.

Kat's embarrassment had only been heightened when a voice spoke up from the curtains that led to the stage. "What would Mom think, Kat? Should I go get her, so she can see what you're really like?" They'd both looked up to see Rachel watching them. Her eyes had been narrowed, those eyes that were so like Kat's but so very, very different. Even then, ten years ago, there hadn't been any confusing the sisters. Only an eighth grader, Rachel hadn't yet resorted to the dyed hair and tattoos that she sported as an adult. But she'd painted heavy black outlines around her eyes, and she wore clunky earrings and half a dozen rings on either hand. Rachel had laughed at her sister then, obviously relishing Kat's embarrassment over that awful mistake of a kiss.

Rachel must not have told, though. There hadn't been any repercussions. And Rye's fumbling obviously hadn't made any lasting impression—Kat hadn't even remembered his name, yesterday at the train station.

Kat stiffened as she heard Rye's voice. A jumble of emotions flashed through her head—guilt, because she shouldn't be caught at the barre, not when she was supposed to be resting her injured foot. Shame, because no one should see the studio in its current state of disarray. Anger, because Rachel should never have let things get so out of hand, should never have left so much mess for Kat to clean up. And a sudden swooping sense of something else, something that she couldn't name precisely. Something that she vaguely thought of as pleasure.

Shoving down that last thought—one that she didn't have time for, that she didn't deserve—she lowered her arm and turned to face Rye. "How did you get in here?"

"The front door was open. Maybe the latch didn't catch when you came in?"

Kat barked a harsh laugh. "That makes one more thing that's broken."

Rye glanced around the studio, his eyes immediately taking in the ceiling leak. "That looks bad," he said. "And the water damage isn't new."

Kat grimaced. "It's probably about six months old."

"Why do you say that?"

"It's been six months since my father got sick. My sister, Rachel, has been running this place and…she's not the best at keeping things together."

Rye fought the urge to scowl when he heard Rachel's name. Sure, the woman had her problems. But it was practically criminal to have let so much water get into a hardwood floor like this one. He barely managed not to shake his head. He'd dodged a bullet with Rachel, seeing through to her irresponsible self before he could be dragged down with her.

But it wasn't Rachel standing in front of him, looking so discouraged. It was Kat. Kat, who had come home to help out her family, giving up her own fame and success because her people needed her.

Rye couldn't claim to have found fame or success in Richmond. Not yet. But he certainly understood being called back home because of family. Before he was fully aware of the fact that he was speaking, he heard himself say, "I can help clean things up. Patch the roof, replace the drywall. The floor will take a bit more work, but I can probably get it all done in ten days or so."

Kat saw the earnestness in Rye's black eyes, and she found herself melting just a little. Rye Harmon was coming to her rescue. Again. Just as he had at the train station the day before.

That was silly, though. It wasn't like she was still the starry-eyed eighth grader who had been enchanted by the baseball star in the lead role of the musical. She hardened her voice, so that she could remind herself she had no use for Eden Falls. "That sounds like a huge job! You'll need help, and I'm obviously in no shape to get up on a ladder." She waved a frustrated hand toward her booted foot.

Rye scarcely acknowledged her injury. "There's no need for you to get involved. I have plenty of debts that I can call in."

"Debts?"

"Brothers. Sisters. Cousins. Half of Eden Falls calls me in from Richmond, day or night, to help them out of a bind. What's a little leak repair, in repayment?"

"Do any of those relatives know anything about plumbing?"

Rye looked concerned. "What's wrong with the plumbing?"

For answer, Kat turned on her heel and walked toward the small restroom. The running toilets sounded louder now that she was staring at them with an eye toward repair. She nodded toward the sink. "There isn't any hot water, either."

Rye whistled, long and low. "This place looks like it's been through a war."

"In a manner of speaking." Kat shrugged. "As I said, my sister's been in charge. She's not really a, um, detail person."

"How have they been holding classes here?" Rye asked. "Haven't the students complained?"

And that's when the penny dropped. Students would

have complained the first time they tried to wash their hands. Their parents would have been furious about the warped floor, the chance of injury.

Kat limped to the office and picked up the maple-coated telephone handset. She punched in the studio's number, relying on memories that had been set early in her childhood. The answering machine picked up immediately.

"We're sorry to inform you that, due to a family emergency, Morehouse Dance Academy will not be offering classes for the spring term. If you need help with any other matter, please leave a message, and one of our staff will contact you promptly."

Rachel's voice. The vowels cut short, as if she were trying to sound mature. Official. Kat's attention zeroed in on the nearby answering machine. "57" flashed in angry red numerals. So much for "our staff" returning messages—promptly or at all.

Kat's rage was like a physical thing, a towering wave that broke over her head and drenched her with an emotion so powerful that she was left shaking. If students hadn't been able to sign up for classes, then no money could possibly come into the studio. Rachel couldn't have made a deposit for months. But the water was still on, and the electricity. Susan must have set up the utilities for automatic payment. Even now, the studio's bank account might be overdrawn.

Susan was probably too stressed, too distracted, to have noticed any correspondence from the bank. Fiscal disaster might be only a pen stroke away. All because of Rachel.

Kat's voice shook with fury as she slammed her hand down on the desk. "I cannot be*lieve* her! How could

Rachel do this? How could she ruin everything that Mama worked so hard to achieve?"

Of course Rye didn't answer. He didn't even know Rachel. He couldn't have any idea how irresponsible she was.

Somehow, though, Rye's silence gave Kat permission to think out loud. "I have to get this all fixed up. I can't let my mother see the studio like this. It would break her heart. I have to get the floor fixed, and the plumbing. Get people enrolled in classes."

"I can do the plumbing myself," Rye said, as calmly as if he had planned on walking into this particular viper's nest when he strolled through the studio door. "I'll round up the troops to take care of the leak. You can get started on the paperwork here in the office, see if you find any more problems."

"You make it sound so simple!"

He laughed, the easy sound filling the little office. "I should. It's my job."

She gave him a confused look. "Job?"

"Believe it or not, I can't make a living picking up stranded passengers at the train station every day. I'm a building contractor—renovations, installations, all of that."

That's right. He'd said something as he handed her the roller bag yesterday, something about Harmon Contracting. Rye was a guy who made the world neater, one job at a time. A guy who made his living with projects like hers. "But didn't Lisa say you were living up in Richmond now?"

A quick frown darted across his face, gone before she was certain she had seen it. "I moved there a month ago. But I've been back in town every weekend. A few more days around here won't hurt me."

What was he saying? Why was he volunteering to spend *more* time in Eden Falls?

Kat wasn't even family. He didn't owe her a thing. What the hell was he thinking, taking on a job like this? More hours going back and forth on I-95. More time behind the wheel of his truck. More time away from the business that he really needed to nurture, from the promise he'd made to himself.

This was Marissa, all over again—a woman, tying him down, making him trade in his own dreams for hers. This was the same rotten truth he'd lived, over and over and over, the same reflexive way that he had set his dreams aside, just because he had the skills to help someone else. Just because he could.

But one look at the relief on Kat's face, and Rye knew he'd said the right thing.

And Harmon Contracting wasn't exactly taking Richmond by storm. He didn't need to be up the road, full-time, every day. And it sure looked like Kat needed him here, now.

She shook her head, and he wasn't sure if the disbelief in her next words was because of the generosity of his offer, or the scale of the disaster she was still taking in, in the studio. "I don't even know how I'll pay you. I can't let my mother find out about this."

"We'll work out something," Rye said. "Maybe some of my cousins can take a ballet class or two."

Kat just stared. Rye sounded like he rescued maidens in distress every day. Well, he had yesterday, hadn't he? "Just like that? Don't we need to write up a contract or something?"

Rye raised a mahogany eyebrow. "If you don't trust me to finish the job, we can definitely put something in writing."

"No!" She surprised herself by the vehemence she forced into the word. "I thought that *you* wouldn't trust *me.*"

"That wouldn't be very neighborly of me, would it?" She fumbled for a reply, but he laughed. "Relax. You're back in Eden Falls. We pretty much do things on a handshake around here. If either one of us backs out of the deal, the entire town will know by sunset." He lowered his voice to a growl, putting on a hefty country twang. "If that happens, you'll never do business in this town again."

Kat surprised herself by laughing. "That's the voice you used when you played Curly!"

"Ha!" Rye barked. "You *did* recognize me!"

Rye watched embarrassment paint Kat's cheeks. She was beautiful when she blushed. The color took away all the hard lines of her face, relaxed the tension around her eyes.

"I —" she started to say, fumbling for words. He cocked an eyebrow, determined not to make things easier for her. "You —" she started again. She stared at her hands, at her fingers twisting around each other, as if she were weaving invisible cloth.

"You thought it would be cruel to remind me how clumsy I was on stage, in *Oklahoma*. That was mighty considerate of you."

"No!"

There. Her gaze shot up, as if she had something to prove. Another blush washed over her face. This time, the color spread across her collarbones, the tender pink heating the edges of that crisp black top she wore. He had a sudden image of the way her skin would feel against his lips, the heat that would shimmer off her as he tasted....

"No," she repeated, as if she could read his mind. Now it was his turn to feel the spark of embarrassment. He most definitely did not want Kat Morehouse reading his mind just then. "You weren't clumsy. That dance scene would have been a challenge for anyone."

"Except for you." He said the words softly, purposely pitching his voice so that she had to take a step closer to hear.

Her lips twisted into a frown. "Except for me," she agreed reluctantly. "But I wasn't a normal kid. I mean, I already knew I was going to be a dancer. I'd known since I was five. I was a freak."

Before he could think of how she would react, he raised a hand to her face, brushing back an escaped lock of her coal-black hair. "You weren't a freak. You were never a freak."

Her belly tightened as she felt the wiry hairs on the back of his fingers, rough against her cheek. She caught her breath, freezing like a doe startled on the edge of a clearing. *Stop it*, she told herself. *He doesn't mean anything by it. You're a mess after one morning spent in this disaster zone, and he's just trying to help you out. Like a neighbor should.*

Those were the words she forced herself to think, but that's not what she wanted to believe. Rye Harmon had been the first boy to kiss her. Sure, she had pretended not to know him the day before. And over the years, she'd told herself that it had never actually happened. Even if it had, it had been a total accident, a complete surprise to both of them. But his lips had touched hers when she was only fourteen—his lips, so soft and sweet and kind—and sometimes it had seemed that she'd been spoiled for any other boy after that.

She forced herself to laugh, and to take a step

away. "We all think we're freaks when we're teenagers," she said.

For just an instant, she thought that he was going to follow her. She thought that he was going to take the single step to close the distance between them, to gather up her hair again, to put those hands to even better use.

But then he matched her shaky laugh, tone for tone, and the moment was past. "Thank God no one judges us on the mistakes we make when we're young," he said.

Rye berated himself as Kat sought refuge behind the desk. What the hell was he doing, reacting like that, to a woman he hadn't seen since she was a kid? For a single, horrible second, he thought it was because of Rachel. Because of those few tumultuous weeks, almost six years before.

But that couldn't be. Despite the DNA that Kat and Rachel shared, they were nothing alike. Physically, emotionally—they might as well live on two different planets. He was certain of that—his body was every bit as sure as his mind.

It was Kat who drew him now. Kat who attracted him. Kat whom he did not want to scare away.

He squared his shoulders and shoved his left hand deep into the pocket of his jeans. "Here," he said, producing a small leather case. "You left your cell phone in my car. I found it this morning, and I called your parents' house, but your mother said you were over here."

Kat snatched the phone from his open palm, like a squirrel grabbing a peanut from a friendly hand. She retreated behind the desk, using the cell as an excuse to avoid Rye's eyes, to escape that warm black gaze. Staring at the phone's screen, she bit her lip when she realized she still had no reception. "Stupid carrier," she said.

"Pretty much all of them have lousy reception around here. It's better up on the bluffs."

The bluffs. Kat may have left town when she was fourteen, but she had already heard rumors about the bluffs. About the kids who drove up there, telling their parents they were going to the movies. About the kids who climbed into backseats, who got caught by flashlight-wielding policemen.

But that was stupid. She wasn't a kid. And it only made sense that she'd get better cell phone reception at the highest point in town. "I'll head up there, then, if I need to make a call."

Damn. She hadn't quite managed to keep her voice even. Well, in for an inch, in for a mile. She might as well apologize now, for having pretended not to know him.

She took a deep breath before she forced herself to meet his eyes. He seemed to be laughing at her, gently chiding her for her discomfort. She cleared her throat. "I'm sorry about yesterday. About acting like I didn't know who you were. I guess I just felt strange, coming back here. Coming back to a place that's like home, but isn't."

He could have made a joke. He could have tossed away her apology. He could have scolded her for being foolish. But instead, he said, "'Like home, but isn't.' I'm learning what you mean." At her questioning look, he went on. "Moving up to Richmond. It's what I've always wanted. When I'm here, I can't wait to get back there, can't wait to get back to work. But when I'm there…I worry about everyone here. I think about everything I'm missing."

It didn't help that everyone in Eden Falls thought he was nuts for moving away. Every single member of his family believed that the little town was the perfect place to raise kids, the perfect place to grow up, surrounded by generations. Marissa had said that to him, over and over again, and he'd believed her, because Eden Falls was the only place he'd ever known.

But now, having gotten away to Richmond, he knew that there was a whole wide world out there. He owed it to himself to explore further, to test himself, to see exactly how much he could achieve.

Like Kat had, daring to leave so long ago. If anyone was going to understand him, Kat would.

He met her gaze as if she'd challenged him out loud. "I have to do it. It's like I…I have to prove something. To my family and to myself—I can make this work, and not just because I'm a Harmon. Not just because I know everyone in town, and my daddy knows everyone, and his daddy before him. If I can make Harmon Contracting succeed, it'll be because of who *I* am. What *I* do."

Kat heard the earnestness in Rye's voice, the absolute certainty that he was going to make it. For just a second, she felt a flash of pain somewhere beneath her breastbone, as if her soul was crying out because she had lost something precious.

But that was absurd. Rye had moved to Richmond, the same way that she had moved to New York. They both had found their true paths, found their way out of Eden Falls. And she'd be back in her true home shortly, back with the National Ballet, back on stage, just as soon as she could get out of her stupid walking boot.

And as soon as she got the Morehouse Dance Academy back on its feet. She pasted on her very best smile and extended her hand, offering the handshake that would seal their deal. "I almost feel guilty," she said. "Keeping you away from Richmond. But you're the one who offered."

His fingers folded around hers, and she suddenly had to fight against the sensation that she was falling, tumbling down a slope so steep that she could not begin to see the bottom. "I did," he said. "And I always keep my word."

His promise shivered down her spine, and she had to remind herself that they were talking about a business proposition. Nothing more. Rye Harmon would never be anything more to her. He couldn't be. Their past and their future made anything else impossible.

Chapter Three

Three days later, Kat was back in the studio office, sorting through a stack of papers. Rye was working in the bathroom, replacing the insides of the running toilets. The occasional clank of metal against porcelain created an offbeat music for Kat's work.

She'd been productive all morning long. That was after seeing Jenny off to school, ignoring the child's demands for sugar on her corn flakes, an extra sparkling ribbon for her hair and a stuffed animal to keep her company throughout the day. Kat had a plan—to bring order to Jenny's life—and she was going to stick with it. If it took Jenny another day or week or month to get on board, it was just going to take that long.

Not that Kat had any intention of still being in Eden Falls in a month.

That morning, Susan had driven her to the studio. When her mother had put the car in Park and taken off her own seat belt, Kat had practically squawked. "You have to get back to Daddy!"

"I can stay away for an hour," Susan had said. "Let me help you here."

"I'm fine! Seriously. There's hardly anything left for me to do." Susan had looked doubtful, until Kat added, "I just want to have a quiet morning. Maybe do a few exercises. You know, I need to keep in shape." Kat was desperate to keep her mother from seeing the devastation inside the studio. "Please, Mama. The whole reason I'm here in Eden Falls is so that you can rest. Take advantage of me while you can. Relax a little. Go back home and make yourself a cup of that peach tea you like so much."

"I *did* want to get your father sitting up for the rest of the morning. He's feeling so much stronger now that he's getting his sleep."

"Perfect!" Kat had said, letting some of her real pleasure color the word. If her father was recovering, then it was worth all the little struggles to get Jenny in line. "Go home. I'll call Amanda to pick me up when I'm done here."

Susan had smiled then. "My little general," she said, patting Kat's hand fondly. "You've got a plan for everything, don't you?"

Planning. That was Kat's strong suit. Over the weekend, she had written up a list of everything that had to be done at the studio, from computer repair to roofing. She had placed her initials beside each item that she was taking charge of, and she'd dashed off Rye's initials next to his responsibilities. A few items—like the computer—needed to be outsourced, but she would take care of them one by one, doing her best to support the Eden Falls economy.

Goals. Strategies. Rules.

Those were the words that had brought her great success over the years. Sure, as a young girl, miles away from home in New York, she had wondered how she would ever succeed at National Ballet. But she had built her own structure, given her life solid bones—and she had succeeded beyond her wildest dreams.

Okay. Not her wildest dreams. Some of her dreams were pretty wild—she saw herself dancing the tortured maiden Giselle, the girl who died when her love was spurned by the handsome Prince Albrecht. Or the playful animation of the wooden-doll-come-to-life in *Coppelia*. Or the soul-wrenching dual roles of the black and white swans in *Swan Lake*.

All in due time, Kat told herself. As soon as she was out of her hated walking boot, she would exercise like a demon. She would get herself back in top dancing form in no time, transform her body into a more efficient tool than it had been before her injury. Goals. Strategies. Rules.

She could do it. She always had before.

Just thinking about her favorite roles made her long for the National Ballet Company. She hadn't spent more than a weekend away from her ballet friends since moving to New York ten years before. Sitting down at the desk in the office, Kat punched in Haley's phone number. Her roommate picked up on the third ring.

"Tell me that they're making you work like dogs, and I'm impossibly lucky to be trapped here in Small Town Hell," Kat said without preamble.

"I don't know what you're talking about," Haley responded with a mocking tone of wide-eyed wonder. "The company has been treating us to champagne and chocolate-covered strawberries. Free mani-pedis, and hot stone massages for all."

"I hate you," Kat said, laughing.

"How are things on the home front?"

"Well, the good news is that my father seems to be doing better."

"I know you well enough to read *that* tone of voice. What's the bad news?"

Where to start? Kat could say that her niece was a brat. That her sister was a lazy, irresponsible waste of an excuse for a grown woman. That the dance studio was falling down around her ears.

Or she could step back and make herself laugh at the mess she'd volunteered to put right. Squaring her shoulders, she chose the latter route. "There's not a single coffee cart on one corner in all of Eden Falls. And they've never heard of an all-night drugstore."

Haley laughed. "I'd send you a care package, but you'll probably be gone by the time it could get there. Any sign of the prodigal daughter?"

"Rachel? Not a hint. As near as I can tell, she actually took off about three months ago."

"Ouch. You guys really *don't* talk to each other, do you? But didn't your mother just tell you last week?"

"Exactly," Kat said grimly, not bothering to recite the hundreds of reasons she didn't keep in touch with her sister. "Mama didn't want to worry me, or so she says." Kat wouldn't have worried about Rachel. Not for one single, solitary second. Getting *enraged* with her, now that was something else entirely....

"Do they have any idea where she is?"

"She sends my niece postcards. The last one arrived two weeks ago, from New Orleans. A picture of a fan dancer on the front, and postage due."

Haley clicked her tongue. "She really is a piece of work, isn't she?"

Kat sighed. "The thing is, I don't even care what she does with her own life. I just hate seeing the effect it has on my parents. And Jenny, too. She's not a bad kid, but she hasn't had any structure in her life for so long that she doesn't even know *how* to be good."

"How much longer are you staying?"

That was the sixty-four-thousand-dollar question, wasn't it? "I'm not sure. At first, I thought that I could only stand a week here, at most."

"But now?"

"Now I'm realizing that there's more work to take care of than I thought there was. Mama's dance studio has been a bit…ignored since Daddy got sick."

"I thought your sister was taking care of all that."

"I'll give you a moment, to think about the logic of that statement." Over the years, Kat had vented to Haley plenty of times about Rachel. "I've got my goals in place, though. Rye should be able to get everything pulled together in another week or so. Ten days at most."

"Rye?" There were a hundred questions pumped into the single syllable and more than one blatantly indecent suggestion. Kat's heart pounded harder, and she glanced toward the hallway where Rye was working.

"Don't I wish," Kat said, doing her best to sound bored. Haley had been intent on making Kat forget about her disastrous relationship with Adam; her roommate had even threatened to set up an online dating profile for her. Haley would be head over heels with the *idea* of Rye Harmon, even though she'd never met the guy. Trying to seem breezy and dismissive, Kat said, "Just one of the locals. A handyman."

But that wasn't the truth. Not exactly. Rye had driven down from Richmond that morning, to take care of the studio's plumbing. And he wasn't just a handyman—he was a contractor. A contractor who was taking her project quite seriously…

"Mmm," Haley said. "Does he have any power tools?"

"Haley!" Kat squawked at the suggestive tone.

"Fine. If you're not going to share any intimate details, then I'm going to head out for Master Class."

A jolt of longing shot through Kat, and she glared at the paneled wall of the studio office. She had really been looking forward to the six-week Master Class session taught by one of Russia's most prominent ballerinas. She pushed down her disappointment, though. It didn't have anything to do with her being trapped here in Virginia. In fact, she would have felt even worse to be out of commission in New York, completely surrounded by an ideal that she couldn't achieve.

"I want to hear all about it!" she said, and she almost sounded enthusiastic for her friend.

"Every word," Haley vowed. They promised to talk later in the week, and Kat cradled the phone.

Her conversation with Haley had left her restless, painfully aware of everything she was missing back home. She wanted to dance. Or at least stretch out at the barre.

But there was other work to complete first. She sighed and sat at the desk, which was still overflowing with coffee-stained papers. Even if Rachel *had* maintained perfect records, they'd be impossible to locate in this blizzard. Tightening her core muscles, Kat got to work.

* * *

Two hours later, she could see clear physical evidence of her hard labor. Raising her chin, Kat clutched the last pile of sorted papers, tapping the edges against the glass surface of the newly cleaned desk. Pens stood at attention in a plastic cylinder. Paper clips were corralled in a circular dish. A stapler and a tape dispenser toed the line, ready to do service. The entire office smelled of lemon and ammonia—sharp, clean smells that spurred Kat toward accomplishing even more of her goals.

Next up: the computer. She had to find out if any of the files could be salvaged, if there was any way to access the hard drive and its list of classes, of students.

She frowned as she glanced at her watch. She could call Amanda and ask for a ride to the tiny computer shop on Main Street. But she was pretty sure Amanda was taking an accounting class over at the community college, taking advantage of her flexible teaching schedule. There was Susan, of course, but Kat wasn't certain that she could deflect her mother again. Susan would almost definitely insist on coming into the studio, and then she'd discover the water damage, the plumbing problems, the utter chaos that Rachel had left behind.

Not to mention the bank account. Kat still dreaded stopping by the bank on Water Street, finding out just how short the studio's account really was.

She sighed. She'd been cleaning up after her sister for twenty-four years. It never got any easier.

Well, there *was* another option for dealing with the computer. There was an able-bodied man working just down the hall. An able-bodied man with a shining silver pickup truck. Firming her resolve, Kat marched down to the bathroom.

She found Rye in the second stall, wedged into an awkward position between the toilet and the wall. He was shaking his head as she entered, and she was pretty sure that the words he was muttering would not be fit for little Jenny's ears—or the ears of any Morehouse Dance Academy students, either. He scowled down at the water cutoff with a ferocity that should have shocked the chrome into immediate obedience.

"Oh!" Kat said in surprise. "I'll come back later."

Rye pushed himself up into a sitting position. "Sorry," he said. "I don't usually sound like a sailor while I work."

"Some jobs require strong language," Kat said, quoting one of the stagehands at the National. "Seriously, I'll let you get back to that. It was nothing important. I'm sorry I interrupted."

"I'll always welcome an interruption from you."

There was that blush again. Rye could honestly say that he hadn't been trying to sweet-talk Kat; he had just spoken the truth, the first thing that came to mind.

That rosy tint on her cheeks, though, made her look like she was a kid. The ice princess ballerina melted away so quickly, leaving behind the girl who had been such an eager dancer, such an enthusiastic artist. He wondered what they had taught her at that fancy high school in New York City. How had they channeled her spirit, cutting off her sense of humor, her spirit of adventure? Because the Kat Morehouse he had known had been quiet, determined, focused. But she had known how to laugh.

This Kat Morehouse looked like she had all the cares of the world balanced on her elegant shoulders. He was pleased that he had made her blush again. Maybe he could even make her smile. A smile would make the whole day worthwhile, balance out the drive down from Richmond, the day spent away from Harmon Contracting business.

"What's up?" he asked, climbing to his feet. The flange was frozen shut. He was going to have to turn the water off at its source, then cut out the difficult piece.

She cleared her throat. It was obviously difficult for her to say whatever she was thinking. "I just wondered if you could drive me down to Main Street. I need to take in the computer, to see if they can salvage anything from the hard drive."

Huh. Why should it be so difficult for her to ask a favor? Didn't people help each other out, up in New York? He fished in his pocket and pulled out his key ring. "Here. Take the truck. That'll give me a chance to talk to this thing the way I really need to."

Kat backed away as if he were handing her a live snake. She knew he didn't mean anything by the casual offer of the keys. He wasn't trying to make her feel uncomfortable, abnormal. But as the fluorescent light glinted off the brass keys, all she could hear was Jenny's querulous voice asking, "But why *can't* Aunt Kat drive?"

She cleared her throat and reminded herself that she had a perfectly good excuse. It would have been a waste of her time to get behind the wheel in New York—time that she had spent perfecting her arabesque, mastering her pirouettes. "I can't drive," she said flatly. She saw a question flash in his eyes, and she immediately added, "It's not like I've lost my license or anything. I never had one."

"Never—" he started to say, but then he seemed to piece together the puzzle. "Okay. Give me a minute to wash up, and we can head there together."

"Thank you," she said, and a flood of gratitude tinted the words. She was grateful for more than his agreeing to run the errand with her. She appreciated the fact that he hadn't pushed the matter, that he hadn't forced her to go into any details.

It felt odd to watch as Rye lifted the computer tower from beneath the desk in the office. It was strange to follow him out to the truck. She was used to being the person who did things, the woman who executed the action plan. But she had to admit she would have had a hard time handling the heavy computer and the studio door, all while keeping her balance with her walking boot.

Rye settled the computer in the back of the truck, nestling it in a bed of convenient blankets. She started to hobble toward the passenger door, but he stopped her with a single word: "Nope."

She turned to face him, squinting a little in the brilliant spring sun. "What?"

"Why don't you get behind the wheel?"

So much for gratitude that he hadn't pressed the issue. She felt iron settle over her tone. "I told you. I don't know how to drive."

"No time like the present. I'm a good teacher. I've taught five siblings."

A stutter of panic rocketed through Kat's gut. She wasn't about to show Rye how incompetent she was, how unsuited to life in Eden Falls. She forced a semblance of calm into her words. "Maybe one of them will drive me, then."

Rye's voice was gentle. Kind. "It's not that difficult. I promise. You don't have to be afraid."

Kat did not get afraid. She leaped from the stage into a partner's arms. She let herself be tossed through the air, all limbs extended. She spun herself in tight, orchestrated circles until any ordinary woman would have collapsed from dizziness. "Fine," she snapped. But her spine was ice by the time she reached the driver's door.

With her long legs, she didn't need to move the seat up. She fastened her seat belt, tugging the cloth band firmly, and she glared at Rye until he did the same. She put her hands on the steering wheel, gripping tightly as she tried to slow her pounding heart. The muscles in her arms were rigid, and her legs felt like boards.

"Relax," Rye said beside her. "You're going to do fine."

"You say that now," she muttered. "But what are you going to say when I crash your truck?"

"I know that's not going to happen."

She wished that she had his confidence. She stared at the dashboard, as if she were going to control the vehicle solely through the power of her mind.

"Relax," he said again. "Seriously. Take a deep breath. And exhale…"

Well, that was one thing she could do. She'd always been able to control her body, to make it do her bidding. She breathed into the bottom of her lungs, holding the air for a full count of five, before letting it go. Alas, the tension failed to flow away.

Rye reached over and touched her right leg. Already on edge, Kat twitched as if he'd used a live electric wire. "Easy," he said, flattening his palm against her black trousers. She could feel the heat of his palm, the weight of each finger. Nervous as she was, she found his touch soothing. Relaxing. Compelling.

Leaving his hand in place, Rye said, "The pedal on the right is gas. The one on the left is the brake. You'll shift your foot between them. You want to be gentle— I told my brothers to pretend that there were eggs beneath the pedals."

He lifted his hand, and her leg was suddenly chilled. She wanted to protest, wanted him to touch her again, but she knew that she was being ridiculous. Any fool could see that she was just trying to delay the inevitable driving lesson.

"Put your foot on the brake," he said. "Go ahead. You can't hurt anything. I promise."

I promise. He was so sure of himself. He had so much faith in her. She wanted to tell him that he was wrong, that he was mistaken, that she didn't know the rules for driving a car. She didn't have a system. Tenuously, though, she complied with the instruction. He nodded, then said, "Good. Now, take this."

She watched him select a key, a long silver one with jagged teeth on either side. He dangled it in front of her until she collected it, willing her hand to stop shaking, to stop jangling all the other keys together. He nodded toward the ignition, and she inserted the key, completing the action after only two false starts.

"See?" he said. "I told you this was easy."

"Piece of cake," she muttered, sounding like a prisoner on the way to her own execution.

Rye chuckled and said, "Go ahead. Turn it. Start the truck."

"I—I don't know how."

"Exactly the same way you open the lock on a door.

You do that all the time, up in New York, don't you? It's the exact same motion."

Tightening her elbow against her side to still her trembling, she bit on her lower lip. Millions of people drove every single day. People younger than she was. People without her discipline. She was just being stupid—like the time that she'd been afraid to try the fish dives in *Sleeping Beauty.*

She turned the key.

The truck purred to life, shuddering slightly as the engine kicked in. Her hand flew off the key, but Rye only laughed, catching her fingers before she could plant them in her lap. He guided them to the gearshift, covering her hand with his own. His palm felt hot against her flesh, like sunshine pooling on black velvet. She thought about pulling her hand away, about blowing on her fingers so that they weren't quite icicles, but she was afraid to call even more attention to herself.

"The truck is in Park. You're going to shift it into Drive." His fingers tightened around hers, almost imperceptibly. The motion made her glance at his face. His black eyes were steady on hers, patient, waiting. "You can do this, Kat," he said, and the words vibrated through her. She didn't know if her sudden breathlessness was because of his touch, or because she was one step closer to driving the truck.

She shifted the gear.

"There you go." He crooned to her as if she were a frightened kitten. "Now, shift your foot to the gas. The truck will roll forward just a little—that's the power of the engine pulling it, without giving it any fuel. When you're ready, push down on the gas pedal to really make it move." He waited a moment, but she could not move. "Come on," he urged. "Let's go."

She looked out the windshield, her heart pounding wildly. "Here?" she managed to squeak.

"We're in a parking lot. There's not another vehicle around. No lights. Nothing for you to hit." He turned the words into a soothing poem.

He was being so patient. So kind. She had to reward his calm expectation, had to show him that his confidence was not misplaced. She tensed the muscles in her calf and eased her foot off the brake. As he had predicted, the truck edged forward, crunching on gravel with enough volume that she slammed back onto the brake.

Rye laughed as he slid his thumb underneath his seat belt, loosening the band where it had seized tight against his shoulder. "That's why they make seat belts," he said. "Try it again."

This time, it was easier to desert the brake. She let the truck roll forward several feet, getting used to the feel of the engine vibrating through the steering wheel, up her arms, into the center of her body. She knew that she had to try the gas pedal next, had to make the silver monster pick up speed. Steeling herself, she plunged her foot down on the gas pedal.

The truck jumped forward like a thoroughbred out of the gate. Panicked, she pounded on the brake, throwing herself forward with enough momentum that her teeth clicked shut.

"Easy, cowboy!" Rye ran a hand through his chestnut curls. "Remember—like an egg beneath the pedal."

She set her jaw with grim determination. She could do this. It was a simple matter of controlling her body, of making her muscles meet her demands. She just needed to tense her foot, tighten her calf. She just

needed to lower her toes, that much…that much…a
little more….

The truck glided forward, like an ocean liner pulling
away from a dock. She traveled about ten yards before
she braked to a smooth stop. Again, she told herself,
and she repeated the maneuver three times.

"Very good," Rye said, and she realized that she'd
been concentrating so hard she had almost forgotten the
man beside her. "Now you just have to add in steering."

She saw that they were nearing the end of the parking lot. It was time to turn, or to learn how to drive in
Reverse. She rapidly chose the lesser of the two evils.
Controlling the steering wheel was just another matter
of muscle coordination. Just another matter of using
her body, of adapting her dance training. Concentrating with every strand of her awareness, she eased onto
the gas and turned the truck in a sweeping circle.

Rye watched Kat gain control over the truck, becoming more comfortable with each pass around the parking lot. He couldn't remember ever seeing a woman
who held herself in check so rigidly. Maybe it was her
dancer's training, or maybe it was true terror about
managing two tons of metal. He longed to reach out, to
smooth the tension from her arms, from the thigh that
had trembled beneath his palm.

Mentally, he snorted at himself. He hadn't lied when
he told her that he'd taught each of his siblings. They'd
been easy to guide, though—each had been eager to
fly the nest, to gain the freedom of wheels in a small
Virginia town.

Suddenly, he flashed on a memory of his own youth-
ful days. He'd been driving his first truck, the one that
he had bought with his own money, saved from long
summers working as a carpenter's apprentice. He'd

just graduated from college, just started dating Rachel Morehouse.

She hadn't been afraid, the way that Kat was. Rachel had tricked him with a demon's kiss, digging into his pockets when he was most distracted. She had taken his keys and run to his truck, barely giving him time to haul himself into the passenger side before she had raced the engine. She had laughed as she sped toward the county road, flooring the old Ford until it shuddered in surrender. Rachel had laughed at Rye's shouted protest, jerking the wheel back and forth, crossing the center line on the deserted nighttime stretch of asphalt. When a truck crested a distant rise, Rachel had taken the headlights as a challenge; she had pulled back into their own lane only at the last possible instant.

He had sworn every curse he knew, hollering until Rachel finally pulled onto the crumbling dirt shoulder. He'd stomped around the truck, glaring as she slid across the bench seat with mock meekness. He'd dropped her back at her house, pointedly ignoring her pursed lips, her expectation of a good-night kiss.

And he'd broken up with her the next morning.

He would never have believed that Rachel and Kat were related, if their faces hadn't betrayed them. Their personalities were opposites—a tornado and an ice storm.

He cleared his throat, certain that his next words would lock another sheet of Kat's iron control into place. "All right. Let's go out on the road." He wasn't disappointed; she clenched her jaw tight like a spring-bound door slamming shut.

"I can't do that," Kat said. It was one thing to drive in an abandoned parking lot. It was another to take the truck out onto the open road. There would be other drivers there. Innocent pedestrians. Maybe even a dog or two, running off leash. She could cause immeasurable damage out on the road.

"The computer store isn't going to come to you." Rye's laugh made it sound as if he didn't have a care in the world. "Come on, Kat," he cajoled when she stopped in the middle of the parking lot. "What's the worst that can happen?"

"A fifteen-car pileup on Main Street," she said immediately, voicing the least bloody of the images that tormented her.

"There aren't even fifteen cars on the road at this time of day. You're making excuses. Let's go."

There. He'd set their goal—she would drive them to the store. She knew the strategies—she needed to put the truck in gear, to turn out onto Elm Street, to navigate the several blocks down to Main. She was familiar with the rules, had observed them all her life: stay on the right side of the road, keep to the speed limit, observe all the stop signs.

At least there weren't any traffic lights, dangerous things that could change from green to red in a heartbeat, with scarcely a stop at yellow.

She took a deep breath and pulled onto Elm.

For the first couple of blocks, she felt like a computer, processing a million different facts, arriving at specific conclusions. She had never realized how many details there were in the world around her, how many things moved. But she completed her first turn without incident. She even followed Rye's instruction when he suggested that she take a roundabout path, that she experiment with more right turns, and a single, terrifying left.

She wasn't thinking when Rye told her to take one

more left turn; she didn't realize that they were on the county road until after the steering wheel had spun back to center. There was oncoming traffic here—a half-dozen cars whooshed by at speeds that made her cringe.

"Give it a bit more gas," Rye said. "You need to get up to forty."

She wanted to yell at him, to complain that he had tricked her onto this dangerous stretch of road, but she knew that she should not divert her attention. She wanted to tell him that forty was impossibly fast, but she knew that he was right. She could see the black-and-white speed limit sign—she presented more of a danger to them, creeping along, than she would if she accelerated. She hunched a little closer to the steering wheel, as if that motion would give her precious seconds to respond to any disasters.

Maybe it was her concentration that kept her from being aware of the eighteen-wheeler that roared by, passing her on the left. One moment, she could dart a glance out at freshly tilled fields, at rich earth awaiting new crops. The next, a wall of metal screamed beside her, looming over her like a mountain. She thought that she was pounding on the brake, but she hadn't shifted her foot enough; the pickup leaped forward as she poured on more fuel, looking for all the world like she was trying to race the semi.

The surge terrified her, and she shifted her foot solidly onto the brake. At the same time, the truck cut back into her lane, close enough that the wind of its passing buffeted her vehicle. Kat overcorrected, and for one terrible moment, the pickup slid sideways across the asphalt road. She turned the wheel again, catching the rough edge of the shoulder, and one more twist sent her careening out of control.

The pickup bucked as it caught on the grass at the roadside, and she could do nothing as the vehicle slid into the ditch at the edge of the road. Finally, the brake did its job, and the truck shuddered to a stop. Kat was frozen, unable to lift her hands from the wheel.

Rye reached across and turned the key, killing the idling motor. "Are you okay?" he asked, his voice thick with concern.

"I'm fine," Kat said automatically. *I'm mortified. I nearly got us killed. I'm a danger to myself and others.* "I'm fine," she repeated. "How about you?"

Rye eased a hand beneath his seat belt once more. "I'm okay."

"I'm so sorry," Kat said, and her voice shook suspiciously. "I don't know how that happened. One minute everything was fine, and then—" She cut herself off. "I could have killed us."

"No blood, no foul," Rye said.

Kat burst into tears.

"Hey," he said. "Come on. You can drive out of this ditch. We don't even need to get the truck towed."

She nodded, as if she agreed with everything he said. At the same time, though, she was thinking that she was never going to drive again. She was never going to put herself in danger—herself or any innocent passenger. What if Susan had been with her? Or Mike, in his weakened state? What if, God forbid, Jenny had been sitting there?

She fumbled for the door handle and flung herself out of the truck. Rye met her by the hood, settling his firm hands on her biceps. "What's wrong?" he asked.

"I can't do this!" Her words came out more a shout than a statement.

"You've just been shaken up. You know the drill—back up on the horse that threw you."

"I'm not a rodeo rider."

"No, but you're a dancer. And I have to believe that you stick with adversity on the stage better than this."

She shook her head. This wasn't dance. This wasn't her career. This was—literally—life or death. She couldn't think of working anymore for the day. "Please, Rye. Will you just drive me back to Rachel's?"

He looked at her for a long time, but she refused to meet his eyes. Instead, she hugged herself, trying to get her breathing back under control, trying to get her body to believe that it wasn't in imminent danger.

At last, Rye shrugged and walked around the cab of the truck, sliding into the driver's seat with a disgruntled sigh. Kat took her place meekly, refusing to look at him as he turned the key in the ignition. The truck started up easily enough, and it only took a little manhandling to get it up the side of the ditch, back onto the road.

Rye knew that he should press the matter. He should make Kat get back behind the wheel. She had to get over her fear. If she walked away from driving now, she'd probably never return.

But who was he to force her to do anything? He was just a guy she'd met ten years before, a guy who lived in Richmond, who kept coming home to a little town in the middle of nowhere, because he couldn't remember how to say no.

Kat was the one who'd had the guts to leave for real. She was the one who'd gone all the way to New York, far enough that it had taken a real disaster to bring her back to Eden Falls. Not the piddling demands that his family made on him day after day.

He tightened his grip on the steering wheel. It had been a mistake to agree to renovate the dance studio. He was building his own life away from Eden Falls. He couldn't let the first woman who'd caught his attention in months destroy his determination to make Harmon Contracting a success.

But he'd already done that, hadn't he? He'd already roped himself into finishing that damned plumbing job. And repairing the ceiling leak wasn't going to be easy, either. And he had a really bad feeling about what he'd find when he really looked at the hardwood floor.

He glanced over at Kat. What did Gran always say? "In a penny, in for a pound." He'd started teaching Kat how to drive, and he'd let her scare herself half to death. She was his responsibility now. It was up to him to convince her to change her mind. To find the nerve to get back in the truck—if not today, then tomorrow. Wednesday at the latest.

He barely realized that he was committing himself to spending half a week away from Richmond.

Kat hopped out as soon as Rye pulled into the driveway. She didn't want to look at the weeds, at the lawn that was impossibly exhausted, even though it was only spring. "Thanks," she said as she slammed her door, and she tried to ignore the hitch in her stride as her boot slipped on the gritty walkway.

Rye didn't take the hint. He followed her to the front door, like a boy walking her home from a date.

Now, why did she think of that image? Rye wasn't her boyfriend. And they most definitely had not been out on a date. Besides, it was broad daylight, the middle of the afternoon.

She opened the unlocked door with an easy twist of her wrist. Not daring to meet his eyes, she pasted a cheery smile on her face. "Thanks for all your help at the studio this morning. Everything's coming along much faster than I thought it would." She stepped back and started to close the door.

Rye caught the swinging oak with the flat of his palm. "Kat," he said, but before he could continue, she saw him wince. He tried to hide the motion, but she was a dancer. She was an expert on all the ways that a body can mask pain.

"You *are* hurt!"

"It's nothing major," he said. "My shoulder's just a little sore from the seat belt."

"Come in here!" She opened the door wide, leaving him no opportunity to demur.

"I'm fine," he said.

She marched him into the kitchen, switching on the overhead light. "Go ahead," she said, nodding. "Take off your shirt. I need to see how bad this is."

Rye shook his head. He was used to his mother clucking over him like a nervous hen. His sisters bossed him around. And now Kat was giving him orders like a drill sergeant. From long experience, he knew he'd be better off to comply now, while he still had some dignity intact. He undid the top two buttons of his work shirt before tugging the garment over his head.

That motion *did* twinge his shoulder, and he was surprised to see the darkening bruise that striped his chest. The seat belt had done its job admirably, keeping him safe from true harm, but he'd have a mark for a few days.

Kat's lips tightened into a frown. "Ice," she said. She turned toward the pantry with military precision, collecting a heavy-duty plastic bag. The freezer yielded enough ice cubes to satisfy her, and then she twisted a cotton dishrag around the makeshift cold pack.

"I don't think—"

"I do." She cut him off. "Believe me, I've had enough bruises that I know how to treat them."

He didn't want to think about that. He didn't want to think about her body being hurt, her creamy skin mottled with evidence of her harsh profession. As if he were accepting some form of punishment, he let her place the ice pack over his chest.

"That's cold," he said ruefully.

"That's the idea." There wasn't any venom in her retort, though. Instead, her hands were gentle as she moved the ice, as she stepped closer, maneuvering the bag until it lay right along his collarbone. The action shifted the midnight curtain of her hair, and he caught a whiff of apricots and honey. Without thinking, he tangled his fingers in the smooth strands, brushing against her nape as he pulled her close. He heard her breath catch in her throat, but she didn't try to edge away. He found her lips and claimed them with his own, a sweet kiss, chaste as schoolkids on a playground.

"There," he whispered against her cheek. "That's a little warmer."

The rasp of his afternoon scruff against her face made Kat catch her breath. Her entire body was suddenly aware of the man before her, aware of him as a *man,* not just a collection of parts that could be manipulated into an entire encyclopedia of ballet poses. Her lips tingled where he had kissed her, ignited as if she had eaten an unexpected jalapeno.

Without making a conscious decision, she shifted her arms, settling into the long lines of his body. She felt his ribs against hers, measured the steady beat of his heart. She matched his legs to her own, shifting her thighs so that she could feel the solid strength of him. He chuckled as he found her lips again, and this time when he kissed her, she yielded to the gentle touch of his tongue.

Velvet against velvet, then, the soft pressure of eager exploration. She heard a sound, an urgent mew, and she realized with surprise that it rose from her own throat. His fingers, tangled in her hair, spread wide and cradled her head. She leaned back against the pressure, glorying in the sensation of strength and power and solid, firm control.

He lowered his lips to the arch of her neck, finding the solid drumbeat of her pulse. One flick of his tongue, another, and her knees grew weak, as if she had danced for an entire Master Class.

Danced. That was what she did. That was what she lived for.

She couldn't get involved with a man in Eden Falls—or Richmond, either, for that matter. She was only visiting; she was heading north as soon as she straightened things out in her parents' home, as soon as Rachel came back to keep an eye on Jenny.

Kat steeled herself and took a step away.

"I think heat might be better than ice for my shoulder," Rye said, a teasing smile on his lips. He laced his fingers between hers.

Those fingers!

Kat remonstrated with herself to focus on what was important. She freed her hand and took another step back. "Ice is better for bruises." She couldn't avoid the confusion that melted into Rye's gaze. "I—I'm sorry," she stammered. "I..." She wasn't sure what to say, didn't know how to explain. "I shouldn't have let myself get carried away."

Carried away. He hadn't begun to carry her away yet.

"I'm sorry," she said again, and this time he heard something that sounded suspiciously like tears, laced beneath her words. "I shouldn't have done that. I'm only here for a few... I can't... I belong in New York."

You belong here, he wanted to say. *Right beside me.* And then he wanted to prove that to her, in no uncertain terms.

But he had no doubt that those words would terrify her. She'd be right back to where she'd been in the ditch—rigid with fear. Rye forced himself to take a steadying breath. To let her go.

"Go ahead," she said after her own shaky breath. "Take the ice pack. You can give me back the towel at the studio, tomorrow."

Rye shrugged, resigning himself to her decision. "Yes ma'am," he said. "But aren't you forgetting something?"

She'd forgotten a lot. She'd forgotten that she was here to help out her parents. Her sister. Her niece. She'd forgotten that she lived in New York, that she had a life—a *career*—far away from Virginia. "What?" she croaked.

"You have a broken computer in the back of my pickup truck."

"Oh!" She hesitated, uncertain of what to do.

"Don't worry," he said, and she sensed that he was laughing at her. "I'll take it down to the shop."

She frowned, and her fingers moved involuntarily toward his shoulder. "But get someone else to lift it out of the truck."

"Yes, ma'am," he said again, but the glint in his eyes said that he was anything but a respectful schoolboy. She showed him to the door before she lost her resolve.

As she heard the truck come to life in the driveway, she shook her head in disbelief. Obviously, she'd been traumatized by her disaster of a driving lesson. She'd been terrified by the thought of dying in a ditch, and the adrenaline had overflowed here in the kitchen. She'd been overtaken by the basest of all her animal instincts.

Well, there was nothing to be done but to rein in those physical responses. Goals. Strategies. Rules. She grabbed a notepad from the drawer beneath the phone and started to revise her schedule for finishing up the studio renovation, for getting all the class records in order for the new term. If she pushed herself hard, she could be out of Eden Falls in one more week.

When she'd finished her schedule, though, she leaned against the counter. Her fingers rose to her lips, starting them tingling all over again. Maybe she'd been too optimistic when she wrote up that list. Seven days wasn't a lot, not to complete everything that needed to be done, and to keep an eye on Jenny, too. Maybe she should plan on staying in Eden Falls a little longer. Ten days. Two weeks. There was no telling *what* might happen in two full weeks.

She laughed at herself as she tore up her list. The renovation would take as long as it took.

And she had to admit—that wasn't a terrible thing. No, it most definitely was not a terrible thing to spend some more time with Rye Harmon. She shook her head and thought about how Haley would tease her when Kat explained why she was staying in Eden Falls a little longer than she had planned at first.

Chapter Four

Kat ushered Susan to the kitchen table, telling her mother to sit down and relax. "You don't need to wait on me like I'm a houseguest," Kat insisted. "I can put the teakettle on to boil."

Still, Susan fussed. "I just want you to rest that foot. You need it to heal, if you're going to get back to New York. Does it still hurt a lot?"

Kat shrugged. She didn't pay a lot of attention to pain. It was all part of her job. She took down two teacups and matching saucers, enjoying the look of the old-fashioned china that had once belonged to her grandmother. "Don't worry about me," she chided Susan. "You have enough on your plate."

"Your father looks so much better. I cannot tell you how much it means, that he's finally able to get a full night's sleep. Jenny is a sweetheart—she's so excited to be reading a book to her Pop-pop right now. But she is a *busy* child."

Busy was one word for her. Spoiled rotten was another. Kat was tired of playing policewoman, constantly telling her niece what to do and what not to do. Just the night before, Kat had caught herself complaining to Haley, saying that Jenny had been raised by wolves. Okay, that was an exaggeration. But not much of one.

But then, just when Kat thought that she had exhausted her last dram of patience with her niece, she was forced to realize that Jenny was just a little girl—a very little girl, who was working through one of the greatest challenges of her short life. Only that morning, after finishing her bowl of corn flakes, Jenny had looked up with such transparent sorrow in her eyes that Kat's heart had almost broken. "When is my mommy coming home?" Jenny had asked.

For once, her lower lip wasn't trembling because she wanted sugary cereal for breakfast, or a plate full of syrupy carbs, or some other disaster for her growing body. Instead, she was trying very hard to be stoic.

Kat had pushed down her own emotions, all of her anger and frustration with Rachel. "Soon," she'd said. "I hope she'll be home soon." She'd given Jenny a brisk hug and then sent her toward the toy chest, telling the child that she needed to collect all the scattered crayons at the bottom of the container, returning them to a plastic bucket neatly labeled for the purpose.

Hard work. That was what had carried Kat through the loneliness and confusion of being on her own in New York. That was the only prescription that she could offer Jenny now.

Standing in Susan's kitchen, Kat rescued the teakettle just before it shrieked. She filled the pot and ferried it over to the table before turning to snatch up a plate of gingersnaps. Somehow, though, her booted foot slipped on the worn linoleum. She caught her balance at the last possible second, but the china plate shattered on the floor.

"Oh, no!" she cried. "I am so sorry! I don't know how I could be so clumsy."

Susan rose from her chair.

"No," Kat cried. "You're only wearing your house shoes! I don't want you to cut your feet. Just sit down." She limped over to the laundry room, quickly procuring a dustpan and broom. Berating herself the entire time, she brushed up the debris, consigning shattered china and dirty cookies to the trash. "Mama, I am so sorry. I can't believe I did that. Here I am, trying to help, and I just make everything worse!"

"Nonsense," Susan said. "It was an accident. Nothing to get so flustered about. Now, sit down, dear, and pour yourself a cup of tea."

Kat complied, strangely soothed by her mother's calm. Susan pushed forward the sugar bowl, but Kat merely shook her head. She hadn't added sugar to her tea since she was younger than Jenny was now.

"Mama, I'll go online. I can find a plate to replace that one—there are websites to help people locate old china patterns."

"Don't worry about it."

"But it belonged to your mother!"

"And she'd be very upset to see you so concerned about breaking it. Please, Kat. Not another word."

Still not satisfied that she'd made appropriate amends, Kat fiddled with her teacup. She avoided her mother's eagle eye as she turned the saucer so that the floral pattern matched the cup precisely.

"I worry about you," Susan said, after Kat had finally taken a sip.

"That's the last thing I want, Mama! I'm here so that you don't have to worry. That's the whole idea!"

"And you're doing wonders, keeping an eye on Jenny and getting everything ready for the first summer classes at the studio."

Kat felt guilty about that. She still hadn't told her mother about the condition of the studio, about the utter lack of students for the spring session. Four times in the past week, she'd started to broach the matter of the bank account, of the money that Rachel had not accounted for during the winter term. Each time, though, Kat had chickened out, dreading the moment when she destroyed her mother's fragile peace of mind. Kat's cowardice was certain to catch up with her. There couldn't be much more time before Susan's life got back to normal, before she found the wherewithal to check her financial statements. Who knew? She might even stop by the columned bank building on Water Street, learn about the disaster firsthand. In public.

And that disaster would be made much worse, because Kat was involved. Kat, whom Susan expected to run things smoothly. Kat, who had never been irresponsible like Rachel. Every day that Kat remained silent was a horrible, festering lie.

She steeled herself to make the admission. After all, if she said something today, then she might still be able to help Susan to recover. Kat could stay on another week or so, help sort out the finances with the help of a sympathetic—or, at the very least, a professional— banker.

She took a deep breath, but Susan spoke before Kat could confess. "Sweetheart, it's *you* that I worry about.

I wish that you could learn to relax a little. To sit back and enjoy life." Susan shook her head, running her finger along the edge of her saucer. "You've always been such a grown-up, even when you were a very little girl. I could leave a slice of pie on the kitchen table, right between you and Rachel, and I always knew that *you* would have the self-restraint to eat your vegetables first." Susan smiled fondly, as if she could still see her twins sitting at her dining room table. "Sometimes, I wish that you still played Magic Zoo."

"Magic Zoo?"

"Don't you remember? It was a game that you invented, to entertain Rachel when she was recovering from that broken arm, the summer when you were six years old. The two of you and your cousin Amanda played it every single day!"

"I have no idea what you're talking about."

"Of course you do! You had all sorts of elaborate rules. Each of you girls chose an animal, and then you drew crayons out of a bucket. Each color crayon corresponded to a different magical food. The foods gave you special powers—you could be a flying horse, or a talking elephant, things like that. The three of you played it for hours on end."

Kat blinked. She had absolutely no recollection of such make-believe games. She couldn't imagine spending "hours on end" with Rachel—not without descending into screaming matches. Maybe Amanda had been a full-time referee?

Susan sighed. "I guess I'm just saying that sometimes you need to be more of a kid. Don't worry as much. Take whatever happens and just roll with it. Forget that you're an adult, for just a little while."

"Like Rachel does, every day." Kat said the words before she could stop herself, but even she was surprised by how bitter they sounded.

Susan's face grew even more serious. "Yes. If I were queen of the universe, I would give Rachel some of your maturity. And I would give you a little of her… what's that phrase? The French one? Joie de vivre?"

"I don't think it's joie de vivre to stay away from home when your own parents, your own *daughter,* need you. When was the last time you heard from Rachel? Do you have any idea when she's planning on coming home?"

"A postcard arrived just yesterday. It had a picture of the Eiffel Tower, but not the real one. She was in Las Vegas. At least that's where the postmark was from."

A postcard, sent what? Three or four days ago? Rachel had to know the phone number here at the house, the one that hadn't changed since they were children. She could have managed to call home, at least once. Responded to the text messages that Kat had sent. She obviously didn't want to be found. She wasn't ready to face up to her adult responsibilities.

Kat fought to keep her voice even. "I'm sure she's very happy there."

"Don't judge your sister," Susan said. "She's never had a skill like yours. She's never known what it means to succeed."

Kat bit back an acid response. Rachel had been given every opportunity Kat had; she had enjoyed the exact same chances in life. Even now, she could come back to Eden Falls, raise her daughter, do the right thing. She could help her parents and prove she was a responsible adult. But she'd rather play in Vegas, drawing out her childhood for countless more years.

Susan sighed. "I sometimes think being twins messed everything up for you girls. Each of you was supposed to get a mixture of responsibility and fun. Of adulthood and childhood. Instead, all the grown-up qualities ended up with you and all the rest…" She let her words drift for a moment, and when she continued she softened her words with a smile. "I want you to have fun, Kat. Go stomping in mud puddles for a change. Somersault down a hill. Don't always think about what something means for your future, for your career."

"Mama, I *need* to worry about my career. I'm a dancer. I don't have much longer to prove myself to the company director."

Susan shook her head. "Sometimes I wonder if we did the right thing, sending you to New York."

"How can you say that?" Kat's voice was etched with horror. She couldn't imagine what her life would have been like without New York. Without dancing.

"Don't look so shocked," Susan murmured. "Your father and I are very proud of you. But sometimes I worry that we took too much away from you by pushing you so hard. You had to grow up so young. You never got a chance to play, to make mistakes. You never even went to your senior prom. We just wanted you to be happy."

"I *was* happy," Kat said. As if to convince herself of the truth behind her words, she went on. "I *am* happy, Mama. The day I stop being happy dancing is the day I'll leave the company. I promise." Susan still looked doubtful. As if to finish the conversation, once and for all, Kat leaned over and gave her mother a hug. "I love you, Mama. You and Daddy, too. And I love everything that you've let me become. Now, can I freshen up your cup of tea?"

She pretended not to see the proud tears glinting in Susan's eyes.

A couple of hours later, after a lunch of tomato soup and grilled cheese sandwiches, Kat could see that her father was tiring. "Come on," she said to Jenny. "Let's go down to the park. Run off some of your energy."

Susan smiled gratefully as she saw them out the door. "Are you sure you're all right walking there?"

"It's only two blocks," Kat assured her. "That's why they call this a walking boot." She made a point of keeping her gait even as they made their way down the street.

When they arrived at the park, it seemed as if half of Eden Falls was taking advantage of yet another unseasonably warm April day. Children screamed with delight on the swings, and a pileup of toddlers blocked the bottom of the slide. A group of teenagers sat beneath a cluster of cherry trees, staring up into the cotton candy blossoms, carrying on a passionate discussion about something.

"What's that?" Jenny said, pointing toward a baseball diamond.

Kat narrowed her eyes against the brilliant sunshine. "A T-ball game."

"I love T-ball!" Jenny bounced on her toes, showing more enthusiasm than she had since Kat had come to town. "Can I play? Please? Please?"

"Let's go see." Kat started across the park, watching Jenny as the child raced ahead. Halfway to the playing field, Kat heard the coach call out, "Good job, Jake! Run! Run to first base!"

Kat knew that voice. She'd listened to it at the dance studio, smiled as it interrupted her organizing class records. She'd imagined it, in her dreams, ever since it had teased her in Rachel's kitchen. She met Rye's gaze as Jenny circled back to clutch at her hand.

"Hey," he said, nodding to include both of them. "Kat. Jenny."

"Hello, Mr. Harmon."

Kat smiled at her niece's polite greeting, and she remembered to model her own good behavior. "Mr. Harmon, Jenny was wondering if she could play T-ball with you."

"Absolutely." Rye gestured toward the outfield. "Go out there, between first and second base. You can play right field for us." Jenny trotted out, beaming as if her most secret wish had been granted.

"Thanks," Kat said, less formal now that none of the kids was paying attention. Her heart was skittering in her chest. It had been, what? Two days since she'd seen Rye? Two days since he had completed fixing the plumbing at the studio, and torn out all the rotten ceiling tiles and the damaged flooring. Two days since he had driven off, with the pair of silent cousins he had brought along to help. Or to serve as chaperones.

As if by agreement, Rye and Kat had made sure they did not spend a minute alone together. Not after that searing kiss they'd shared. Not after Kat had reminded herself that she had no time for an Eden Falls relationship.

She had to clear her throat before she could ask, "What are you doing down here? I thought you went back to Richmond Wednesday night!"

Of course he'd gone back to Richmond. He'd gone back to his rented office, to two beige rooms that had somehow shrunk while he'd been in Eden Falls. He'd gone back to his studio apartment, to a bachelor pad that should have been more than adequate for his needs.

He hadn't slept at all that night.

Every time he rolled over, he imagined having another conversation with Kat. Every time he punched his pillow into a more comfortable lump, he remembered another detail of the studio renovation. Every time he threw off his blankets, he thought about how he had let Kat down with the driving lesson, how she had panicked. And how she had warmed to him, afterward.

No.

It had taken him years to fight his way free, to sever enough family ties, enough social obligations, to give himself permission to live and work in Richmond. That whole mess with Marissa—the way he had pinned his hopes on her, on the life he thought they would have together... A white picket fence, two perfect kids and a dog. Until she decided that Hollywood was more glamorous, and she dropped him like a hot potato.

He might have taken too long to come to his senses, but he had finally carved out a life for himself. He could not—*would* not—let a woman drag him back to Eden Falls. Not now. Not when everything was about to break big for him.

Even a woman as intriguing as Kat. *Especially* a woman as intriguing as Kat. Part of her mystique was the fact that she didn't belong in his hometown. After ten years of living on her own, she had become a New Yorker, through and through. She'd be leaving, as soon as her father had recovered.

He'd be an idiot to forfeit his own life plans—again—for a woman who wasn't going to stick around.

But damn, Kat managed to distract him. Over and over again, even when she was a hundred miles away. And now? Standing beside her at the T-ball bleachers? It was all he could do not to cup a hand around her jean-clad hip. All he could do not to twist a strand of her mesmerizing hair around his finger and make a joke or two, draw out a smile on her lips. All he could do not to forget that a couple dozen kids were clamoring on the baseball diamond behind him, waiting for him to step up to the plate as their dedicated coach.

He cleared his throat and answered Kat's question, even though it seemed like a century had passed since she spoke. "I *was* up in Richmond. But something came up, and my brother Noah had to bail on T-ball practice."

"That seems to happen a lot," Kat said, remembering that Rye had filled in for Noah on her first day back in Eden Falls. "Nothing serious, I hope?"

"Her name is Britney."

Kat laughed. "You're a good brother."

"I'm keeping a log. So far he owes me 327 hours of favors. I get gas money and double credit for Saturdays."

"Oh, what else would you be doing today?"

"I'd find something to occupy my time," he said, giving her an appraising glance. There was no mistaking the rumble beneath his words, and her memory flashed back to the feel of him holding her, to the scratch of his jaw as he kissed her. She felt her cheeks grow warm.

"Mr. Harmon!" one of the kids called. "When do we start to play?"

Rye sighed in fake exasperation, careful to keep the

team from hearing him. "Duty calls. And you're going to have to help out, if we let Jenny play."

She gestured to her boot. "I don't think I'm really up to umpire work."

"I've got that covered. Your place is on the bench, behind home plate. Behind me. You get to be head cheerleader."

Kat caught a flicker of Rye's eyebrows, a comic leer as if he were envisioning her in a short skirt, carrying pom-poms. The expression was wiped away before she could even be certain he was teasing her. Laughing, she headed over to her seat, grateful to give her foot a rest.

Enjoying the fresh air outside the studio and—truth be told—the view of Rye's denim-clad backside behind home plate, Kat put her elbows on the bench above her. Stretching out like a long black cat in the heat of the spring sun, she closed her eyes and leaned her head back. She filled her lungs with the aroma of fresh-cut grass, focusing on what Rye was saying to his young players.

He helped one little girl choke up on the bat, instructing her on how to spread her legs for a more balanced stance. The child was not a natural athlete, but he talked her through two wildly missed swings. On the third, she toppled the ball from its plastic stand. "Run, Kaylee!" he shouted. "Run to first! You can make it!"

His enthusiasm for his charges was obvious. Each child improved under his tutelage. Everyone eventually connected the bat to the ball, and some even got a shot past the infield. Soon enough, the teams switched sides, and Kat watched as Jenny came to the plate.

"Okay, Jenny," Rye said. "Oh, you're left-handed? No, don't be embarrassed, I'm left-handed, too. Here, move to the other side of the plate. Now, Jenny—"

"I'm not Jenny."

Kat sat up, wondering what devilment her niece was working now.

"Really?" Rye said. "I was certain that your Aunt Kat told me your name was Jenny."

"I hate that name." Kat started to climb to her feet, ready to tell Jenny to adjust her tone or they'd be heading back home immediately. Before she could speak, though, the little girl whined pitiably, "There are two other Jennys in my class."

Rye nodded. "I guess that would be pretty annoying. I never had anyone else with my name in school. Should I call you Jennifer instead?"

The little girl shook her head. "I'm only Jennifer when I'm in trouble."

Kat started to laugh—her niece was only telling the truth. Rye, though, screwed up his face into a pensive frown. "What should we do, then? How about another nickname?"

"Like what?"

"Jen?"

"There's a Jen at Sunday School."

"Then how about Niffer?"

"Niffer?" She repeated the name like she'd never heard the last two syllables of her own name.

"Do you know anyone else called Niffer?" The child shook her head. "Then what do you say? Should we try it?" Rye was granted a grudging nod. "Okay, then, Niffer. Step up to the plate. Nope, the other side, for lefties. Now focus on the ball. Bring the bat back. And *swing!*"

The bat cracked against the ball, clearly the best shot of the afternoon. The tiny center fielder scrambled to catch the soaring ball, fighting the sunshine in his eyes. Rye shouted, "Go Niffer! Run around the bases!"

Fulfilling her role as head cheerleader, Kat was shouting by the time her niece completed her home run. The kids exploded with excitement, too, both the batting and the fielding teams chanting, "Nif-fer! Nif-fer!"

Obviously recognizing a climactic ending for the game when he saw one, Rye declared the practice over five minutes early, sending the kids off with their appreciative parents. Kat sat up straighter on the bench, watching Rye talk to the other adults. Several ribbed him about filling in for Noah, one telling him that he was taking his best man's duties too far. So, things must be really serious between Noah and…what was her name? Britney.

Rye was absolutely at home with every person he talked to. He shook hands with all the men; he accepted kisses on the cheek from most of the women. Kat supposed that he'd known these people all his life—he had gone to school with them, grown up with them.

She'd gone to school with them, too. Well, four years behind. She should have been every bit as comfortable in Eden Falls as Rye was. After all, how many places were left on earth where someone could leave her front door unlocked to go play T-ball in the park? How many places would band together to fill Susan and Mike's freezer with countless nourishing, home-cooked meals?

Kat was beginning to understand what had kept her parents here all these years. She even caught herself smiling as Rye crossed the diamond, Jenny at his heels.

"Aunt Kat!"

"You looked great out there, Jenny."

"I'm Niffer, now!"

"Niffer," Kat agreed, sternly reminding herself to use the new nickname.

"Can I go climb on the castle?"

"*May* I?" Kat reminded. Grammar rules were just as important as the other rules that Niffer needed to maintain while they lived together.

"*May* I go climb on the castle?"

"Go ahead," Kat said. "But we need to go back to Gram and Pop-pop's house in ten minutes."

Niffer was halfway to the jungle gym before all of the words were out of Kat's mouth. Rye settled on the bench beside her, grunting with mock exhaustion. "They'll wear a man out."

"You're great with them," Kat said. "I never know how to talk to kids."

"Most people think about it too much. It's better to just say what you're thinking."

"Easy for you! I've been living with…Niffer for a week and a half, and that's the first I heard that she didn't like her name. It's like you two share some special bond."

Special bond. Rye tensed at the words and the responsibility that they conjured up. Years ago, he'd worried about just such a "special bond," worried that the then-unborn Niffer was his daughter. Rachel had set him straight in no uncertain terms. If any guy shared a "special bond" with Niffer, with Rachel, it was Josh Barton.

And just as well. Rye could never have taken off for Richmond if he had a daughter here in Eden Falls. The games that Marissa had played, tying him to the town, would have been nothing compared to the bonds of fatherhood.

"She's a good kid," he finally said.

His lingering tension was telling him something, though. His lingering tension, and a couple of sleepless nights. Even if he had no hope for anything long-term with Kat, it was time to man up. Past time, actually. He flashed on the feel of her body pressed close to his in Rachel's kitchen, and he cleared his throat before saying gruffly, "I should tell you. Your sister and I went out a couple of times. It was a long time ago. Five, six years. We were only together for a few weeks."

Kat's face shuttered closed. "Rachel never mentioned anything. We, um, we haven't been close for a very long time."

Rye wanted to kick himself for making Kat pull away like that, for bringing out that guarded look in her eyes. Over the past few days, he'd relived that kitchen kiss so many times. He'd remembered the swift surge of passion that had boiled his blood as Kat settled her body against him, as her lips parted beneath his. Back in Richmond, he'd picked up the phone a half-dozen times, just wanting to hear her voice. Hell, he'd even grabbed his keys once, thinking about making the drive south in record time.

And he had to admit that he'd wondered—more than once—if she would bring that same sudden passion to his bed. He'd imagined her shifting above him, concentrating on their bodies joined together, fulfilling at last the promise that he'd made with a blushing kiss ten years before.

He was being an idiot, of course. He wasn't going to see Kat in his bed. He was going to honor her clearly stated desire, keep his distance, and finish up his work at the studio. Get the hell out of Eden Falls, and back to Richmond, where he belonged. That was the professional thing to do. The gentlemanly thing to do.

Damn. Sometimes, he hated being the good guy.

Still, his family had dragged him down here for the weekend, and he'd be an idiot not to take advantage of the fact that Kat was sitting right beside him. He just had to reassure her. "It was nothing serious, Kat. Rachel and me."

"With Rachel, it never is."

"She was really interested in another guy, a fraternity brother of mine. After about a month, we both realized the truth, and that was it."

"Of course."

Kat heard the stiffness in her tone. She knew that she had pulled away from Rye as soon as he mentioned Rachel. She was holding her back straight, as if she were about to spin away in a flawless pirouette.

She hated talking about her sister. She hated going over the poor choices Rachel had made, the easy ways out that she'd taken, over and over and over again. Just thinking about the old battles made Kat freeze up, clutching at her old formula—goals, strategies, rules. That's what she needed, here in Eden Falls. That's what she needed throughout her life.

But what had Susan told her, just that morning? *Go stomping in mud puddles for a change. Somersault down a hill.*

Impossible. Mud and hills were both in short supply, here in the public park. But Kat *could* let herself go. Just a bit.

"I'm sorry," she said, forcing herself to relax. "I really do appreciate your telling me about Rachel."

He continued to look grave, though. Her natural reaction had driven a wedge between them. But she could change that—even with stomping and somersaults off the menu for the day. Consciously setting aside her anger with Rachel, Kat dug her elbow into Rye's side. "Come on! I'd race you to the far end of the park, but I'm pretty sure you'd win."

He looked at her walking boot. "Yeah. I wouldn't want to take unfair advantage. What do you think, though? Could you manage the swings?"

"That's about my top speed, these days."

She took the hand that he offered, letting him pull her to her feet. They fell into step easily as they crossed to the swing set. She actually laughed as he gestured toward the center leather strap, waving his hand as if he were presenting her with a royal gift. "Mademoiselle," he said, holding the iron chains steady so that she could sit.

She settled herself gracefully, pretending that the playground equipment was some elegant carriage. Her fingers curled around the chains, and he sat next to her. Neither of them pushed off the scraped dirt, though. Instead, they braced their feet against the ground and continued talking.

"I feel terrible," she said, throwing her head back to look up at the clear blue sky. "Keeping you working in the studio when you should be up in Richmond."

"You shouldn't. A job's a job."

"But this job is taking so much of your time. What do you need, up in Richmond? What am I keeping you from doing?"

Sleeping, he wanted to say. *Concentrating on my work. Focusing on running a business instead of imagining what would have happened if I hadn't let you chicken out the other night.*

"I need to build a website," he said, somehow keeping his voice absolutely even. "Order business cards.

Envelopes. Stationery for bids. I'm lousy at that sort of stuff."

She nodded, as if she were writing down every word. "What else?"

"I've joined the Chamber of Commerce, but I haven't made it to a meeting yet. I've got to get the ball rolling with a little in-person networking. Start building that all-valuable word of mouth."

"That all sounds manageable."

"I've got some paperwork that I have to file with the state. Copies of my license, that sort of thing."

"I've got to say, Mr. Harmon. It sounds like you've got everything pretty much under control. Even *if* I keep dragging you back to Eden Falls."

"I'm glad one of us thinks so." He smiled, to make sure that she didn't take offense. It was his own damn fault that he couldn't stay away from here. His own damn fault that he put thousands of miles on the truck, wearing the tires thin on constant trips up and down the interstate. Old habits died hard.

Time to change the topic of conversation. Time to get away from the way he had screwed up his business plans, over and over and over again, ever since he'd graduated from college.

"So," he said, purposely tilting his voice into a light-hearted challenge. "What do you think? Who can pump higher, here on the swings?"

For answer, Kat laughed and pushed off, bending her knees and throwing back her head. Before he could match her, though, the bells on the courthouse started to toll, counting out five o'clock.

"Wait!" Kat said, stopping short. "Niffer and I have to get home. Mama will start to worry."

He bit his tongue to keep from cursing the bells.

Kat looked around the park, surprised to see that nearly everyone else had left. Of course, it was a Saturday in Eden Falls. Everyone had an early-bird dinner waiting at home. She glanced toward the castle jungle gym, ready to call Niffer and leave.

Except Niffer was nowhere to be seen.

Kat shook her head, forcing herself to swallow the immediate bile of panic. Of course her niece was on the playground equipment. She'd headed over there just a few minutes before.

Kat scrambled to her feet, taking off at a lopsided jog toward the castle. "Niffer!" she called. And then, "Jenny! Jenny!" The bright pink climbing bars mocked her as she reached the base of the toy. Up close, it looked impossibly tall, far too dangerous to be sitting in a public park. "Jenny!"

She looked around wildly. This couldn't be happening. She couldn't have lost her niece. She couldn't have let anything happen to Niffer, to Jenny, to Rachel's daughter.

"Kat! What's wrong?"

Rye skidded to a stop beside her, his ebony eyes flashing. She tried to pull up words past the horror that closed her throat, over the massive wave of guilt. He put a hand on her back, spread his fingers wide, as if to give her a web of support. She started to pull away— she didn't deserve to be touched. She was too irresponsible for anyone to stand near her. She had been given one single goal—watch Jenny—and she had broken all the rules by letting the child wander off unsupervised. Broken all the rules, just so that she could sit on the swings and flirt with Rye Harmon.

Broken all the rules, like Rachel.

"I can't find her," she sobbed. "I told her that she

could go to the castle, and I only looked away for a couple of minutes, but she's gone!"

Without thinking, Rye moved his hand from Kat's back, twining his fingers around hers. He felt her trembling beside him, understood that she was terrified as she darted her gaze around the park. She wasn't seeing anything, though. She was too frightened. No, beyond frightened. Panicked. Not thinking clearly.

He narrowed his eyes, staring into the deep shadows by the oak trees on the edge of the park. There! In the piles of leaves, left over from last autumn. Niffer was plowing through the dusty debris, obviously pretending that she was a tractor, or a dinosaur, or some imaginary creature.

"Look," he said to Kat, turning her so that she could see the child. "She's fine."

Kat stiffened the instant that she saw her niece. Instinctively, Rye tightened his grip on her hand, letting himself be dragged along as Kat stumbled across the uneven grass to the oak tree border.

"Jennifer Allison Morehouse, just what do you think you're doing?"

The little girl froze in midswoop, guilt painting her face. Instead of answering her aunt, though, she turned to Rye. "See? I told you that Jennifer is a bad name."

Incredibly, Kat felt Rye start to laugh beside her. He managed to wipe his face clear after only a moment, but he was standing close enough that she could feel his scarcely bridled amusement. For some reason, his good humor only stoked her anger. "I asked what you are doing over here, young lady! Didn't I give you permission to play on the castle? Not under the trees?"

The child's lower lip began to tremble. "I *was* playing on the castle. I was a princess. But the unicorn mermaids told me that I had to find their diamond ring over here."

Unicorn mermaids. Like Kat was going to buy that. She filled her lungs, ready to let her niece know exactly what she thought of unicorns and mermaids and diamond rings.

Before she could let loose, though, Rye squeezed her hand. Just a little. Barely enough that she was certain she felt it. Certainly not enough that Niffer could see.

Kat remembered her mother, sitting in the drab kitchen, sipping her cooling tea and saying that Kat should be more playful. She remembered Rye coaching the children, encouraging each of them in whatever they did best. She remembered the relaxed camaraderie of the T-ball parents, picking up their kids.

She took a deep breath and held it for a count of five. She exhaled slowly, just as she had when Rye taught her how to drive. No. Not like that. That had ended in disaster.

This was a new venture. A new effort to achieve a different goal. "You'll have to teach me about the unicorn mermaids," she said. "But that will be another day. Right now, we have to get home to Gram and Pop-pop."

Niffer looked as if she thought a magician might have somehow enchanted her Aunt Kat, turned her into a newt, or something worse—a bewitched, unreliable adult. "Okay," she said uncertainly.

"Come on, then," Kat said. "Let's go."

As Niffer started scuffling through the leaves, Kat caught a harsh reprimand at the back of her throat. Instead, she whispered to Rye under the cover of the rustling, "She scared me."

"I know," he whispered back, and he squeezed her hand again.

"She really, really scared me."

"But she's fine," he said. "And you will be, too."

Kat had to remind herself to breathe as they walked out of the park and down the block to her parents' house. Somehow, she forgot to reclaim her hand from Rye's.

Chapter Five

Kat raised her voice over the band, practically shouting so that Amanda could hear her. The crowd was raucous at Andy's Bar and Grill that night, and the musicians were making the most of having a full house. "Okay," she shouted. "You win! You said the music was great and I didn't believe you!"

Amanda laughed and clinked her mug of beer against Kat's. "Drink up!"

Kat obliged. After all, a bet was a bet. This mug tasted even better than the first had.

Kat couldn't remember the last time she'd had so much fun on a Friday night. Amanda had called her around noon, reporting that she'd already arranged for Susan and Mike to keep an eye on Niffer for the evening. Her cousin had picked her up at Rachel's house, only to frown when Kat answered the door in her skinny black jeans and a silk T-shirt. They'd made an emergency stop back at Amanda's house—Kat still wore black, but Amanda had rounded out the outfit with a flame-red scarf, lashed around Kat's hips like a belt. That, and a ruby-drop necklace that had belonged to their grandmother made Kat feel like she was someone new. Someone daring. Someone who wasn't afraid of being a little bit sexy, on a Friday night out on the town.

In fact, when Kat was hanging out with Amanda at the crowded bar, listening to her cousin's running commentary about the cute blond bartender, she felt like she was discovering a whole new world of fun. What had Susan said, the week before? That Kat had been cheated out of going to prom? Maybe Kat *had* lost out on a thing or two in New York, if this was what it felt like to hang out with her cousin, to cut loose, without a care in the world.

Kat certainly couldn't remember the last time she had indulged in drinking alcohol, anything more than a sip or two of champagne at an opening-night gala. Her entire body thrummed in time to the crashing music, and the roof of her mouth had started to tingle. Amanda, on the other hand, seemed entirely unaffected by the single glass of beer that she had sipped.

Before Kat could challenge Amanda to keep pace properly, a man shuffled over to the table. "Hey, Amanda," he said, mumbling a little and looking down at his boots.

"Hey," came Amanda's cool reply. "Brandon Harmon, don't be rude. You remember my cousin Kat, don't you?"

"Hey, Kat," the man said, still intent on studying the floor.

Brandon Harmon. Kat blinked hard and looked at

him as closely as she dared. Nope. She didn't remember him. This being Eden Falls, though, they had probably sat next to each other in fourth-grade social studies. From his name, he had to be one of Rye's countless siblings. Or cousins. Or whatever. It seemed like they comprised half the town.

As if he could read Kat's mind, Brandon looked over his shoulder. There was a cluster of men standing at the bar, their broad shoulders, chestnut curls and midnight eyes all proclaiming them part of the same clan.

Rye stood in the center of the bunch. He lifted his mug toward Kat in a wry salute. She was surprised by the sudden rush of warmth she felt at his attention. Unconsciously, she flexed her fingers, thinking about how strong his hand had felt in hers the Saturday before, after she had panicked about losing Niffer in the park. She'd spent the better part of the past week thinking about Rye's touch. His touch, and the patient humor in his voice… And that truly spectacular kiss that they had shared in Rachel's kitchen…

Kat's belly swooped in a way that had absolutely nothing to do with the beer that she had drunk. She'd felt the same sensation a hundred times in the past week. The past week, while Rye had been working up in Richmond. In between taking care of Niffer and running some errands for Susan, Kat had put in a lot of hours at the studio, but Rye had been nowhere in sight. The hardwood for the new floor had been delivered, though. It needed to spend a week acclimating to the temperature and humidity in the studio. A week when Rye had tended to other business. A week that Kat had been left alone with her memories, with her dreams.

But she was being ridiculous, mooning around, missing Rye. She knew perfectly well that he lived in Richmond now, that he was never moving back to Eden Falls.

And what did it matter? *She* had already spent two weeks in Eden Falls—seven days longer than she'd planned. It was time to turn her attention back to New York. Back to her career. She couldn't daydream about the way Rye's lips quirked just so when he smiled....

In front of her, Brandon shifted his weight from one foot to the other. "Amanda," he said, apparently summoning the nerve to bellow over the music. "Do you want to dance?"

Amanda laughed. "I'm sorry, Brandon. I can't leave my cousin here alone."

The poor man looked so crushed that Kat immediately took pity on him. She feared that he might never screw up his courage to ask out another woman again if she didn't free Amanda now. "Go ahead," she shouted to her cousin. "I'll be fine."

"Really?"

"Go! It's not like I can join you!" Kat gestured at her walking boot.

Amanda laughed and cast a quick glance toward Kat's mug, as if questioning her cousin's judgment. Kat shook her head. She wasn't drunk—not exactly. But she was definitely feeling...relaxed. Loose. Free, in a way that she hadn't felt since coming to Eden Falls. That she hadn't felt in *years*.

As Amanda mouthed a quick "Thank you" from the dance floor, Kat realized just how much her cousin had hoped Kat would let her go. Curious, Kat studied the cowboy, surprised to see how quickly he gained the confidence to place his hands on Amanda's trim waist, to guide her into a smooth Texas Two-Step.

There was something about those Harmon men....

Something about a Southern gentleman with the determination to go after something that he wanted… She swallowed hard, thinking once again of a very different Harmon. She wished that she and Amanda had been drinking soda, or sweet tea, or anything that came in a tall glass with ice, so that she could cool the pulse points in her wrists.

"You're a kind woman," Kat heard, close to her ear. She whirled to find herself face-to-face with Rye.

"What do you mean?" He was close enough that she barely needed to raise her voice. Thank heavens the band was playing, though. Otherwise, he would have heard her heart leap into high gear.

"It took Brandon two whiskey shots to get up the courage to ask Amanda to dance. If you hadn't let her go, all that booze would have gone to waste."

Kat laughed and said, "False courage for a silver-tongued devil like that?" As if to emphasize her words, she set the flat of her palm against Rye's broad chest. The action seemed to surprise him almost as much as it did her—he stiffened at the touch for just a moment. She tossed her hair, though, and thought, *What have I got to lose?* She continued in her best imitation of a carefree flirt. "Why, I bet that Brandon could have any woman in this place."

"Really?" Rye lowered his voice and stepped closer to Kat. He practically nuzzled her neck as he said, "*Any* woman?" She shivered, a delicious trembling that made him think truly evil thoughts. "Come on," he said. "Let's get some fresh air."

"I can't leave Amanda!"

He cupped his hands around his mouth and bellowed, "Hey, Amanda!" When the woman looked up from the dance floor, he pointed once to Kat, once to himself, and once to the door. Amanda laughed and nodded, waving goodbye to both of them. Rye settled one hand on the small of Kat's back as he guided her through the crowd.

A cool evening breeze hit them like an Arctic blast. "Come here," he said, pulling her around the corner of the building. They were sheltered from the wind there, and from the prying eyes of new arrivals to the bar. A bench was pushed up against the rough wooden wall. He gestured toward it and waited for Kat to take a seat. Before she had fully settled, he sat beside her, closer than was strictly necessary.

She wore some sort of sleek black top, one that revealed every bit as much of her figure as it covered, even with its long sleeves. The neckline swooped down, way down, reminding him of the sensitive hollow at the base of her throat. That patch of vulnerable flesh was now marked by a sparkling ruby pendant—as if he could forget it. His fingers twitched, and he resisted the urge to pull at the matching crimson scarf around her waist.

Shivering in the twilight air, Kat rubbed her hands against her arms. "I bet this is where you take all your women." She surprised him for the second time that night, squirming closer to his side, as if she wanted to soak up every ounce of his body heat.

"Just the ones I want to hear talk," he said, yawning a little in a useless attempt to clear the dullness from his ears. Andy's joint was always fun on Friday nights, but the band was far too loud.

"Talk," Kat purred, placing a hand on his thigh. "Is that why you asked me outside?"

This was a Kat he hadn't seen before. Sure, she'd let him kiss her in Rachel's kitchen. And it had seemed second nature to take her hand when she was so worried about Niffer. He'd enjoyed that feeling, that closeness, that sense of protecting her, and he hadn't let go as he walked her back to Susan and Mike's house.

He'd spent the week up in Richmond, though. A week of business. Of remembering his priorities. With his contractor's license properly filed and a dozen business meetings completed, he was newly charged with determination to make Harmon Contracting a success.

Except... Now that he was away from the office? Back in Eden Falls? And breathing in Kat's intoxicating scent...?

Her fingers started to move in distracting patterns, tracing the double-stitched seam on his jeans as if she'd glimpsed his dreams all week long. His body leaped to immediate attention, and he barely swallowed a groan. He leaned forward and found her face already tilted toward him, her lips eagerly parted for his kiss. Heat rolled through him as he breathed in the honey apricot of her hair. He tangled one hand in the lush strands, using the other to trace the shape of that incredible, clinging black top.

He outlined her lower lip with the tip of his tongue, grinning as he heard a needy moan gather at the back of her throat. Her hands were working their own magic, one fiddling with the top button of his shirt, the other continuing its exploration of his increasingly tented jeans. "Kat," he breathed, and then he sealed their kiss.

Heat, and slick velvet, and a pounding, urgent need. But behind that, under her sweet cry, he tasted the sharp bite of hops. Beer. He was shocked to realize that she'd been drinking. Sure, she was an adult; she was allowed to drink alcohol. But his mind refused to reconcile the notion of Kat, the ice princess, cutting loose. Kat, the tightly bound queen of control, tossing back a couple.

All of a sudden he understood the boldness in her hands, the brazen teasing in her words.

He shifted his hand from the back of her head, stopped crushing her close. Instead, he brought his palm around to cup the line of her jaw, using the motion to soften the end of his plunging kiss. She pulled back, just enough for him to look into her platinum eyes. He asked, "How much have you had to drink?"

She looked confused. "Just a couple of beers."

A couple of beers. With her frame? And he was willing to bet that she didn't have any tolerance at all—she couldn't possibly make a practice of hanging out at bars, pounding down a few brewskis on a Friday night.

He leaned in for another kiss, this one quick. Chaste.

"What?" she protested. "I'm an adult. I'm allowed to have a couple of beers."

"Of course you are. But I'm not going to take advantage of you like this."

"It's not taking advantage if I want it, too."

Her blustering response made him certain he was making the right decision. The Kat he knew would never throw herself at him like that. What had she told him, one of those days when he was hanging out at the dance studio? She had *goals* and *strategies* and *rules*.

He clenched his jaw and pulled away from her. "Come on," he said, keeping his voice as light as possible. "Let's get something to eat."

Kat shivered, freezing now that Rye had pulled away from her. She plucked at the scarf around her waist, suddenly ashamed. Two lousy beers. How much could that have impaired her judgment?

But the world was just starting to swirl around the

edges—not enough to make her dizzy, but more than enough to tell her she was over her limit. She thought about what she had done, about where her hands had just been, and she was overwhelmed with a scarlet wash of embarrassment.

"Kat?" Rye's voice was gentle. "Let's go get some dinner at the Garden Diner."

"I don't want dinner," she whispered.

"What? You're going to tell me that dinner goes against your dancer rules?"

More than fooling around on a bench outside a backroads bar? he meant. Her eyes shot up at the amusement in his voice, and her shame started to morph into anger. "What about you?" she challenged him. "Did it take you a couple of shots to come over and talk to me, just like Brandon? I bet you shouldn't be driving around Eden Falls right now."

"I don't need liquor to help me do what I want to do," Rye said. She heard the passion behind his words, the absolute certainty that he *had* wanted to talk to her, to be with her. Even if he'd been gone for the entire week. Even if he'd been the one to pull back just now. His voice was only marginally less fierce as he said, "I stuck to soda water tonight. I have an early day tomorrow, back up in Richmond. A site visit for a prospective client."

Ashamed of her actions all over again, she shook her head and hugged herself, trying to ignore the incipient spinning of the world around her.

"Come on, Kat. You're the one who said you're an adult. Let's be adults together." She flashed him a mortified glance. "Let's go get something to eat," he clarified.

She sighed and let him pull her to her feet. One

single step, though, on the gravel footpath, and she found that her balance was compromised by the damn walking boot. What had she been thinking, betting Amanda about the band, drinking that second beer?

She let Rye slip an arm around her waist, helping her to his truck. At least there was no question of his demanding that she drive tonight. That was one reason that she could actually thank Amanda. She closed her eyes in mortification as Rye reached across her to work her seat belt.

He made small talk as he drove to the diner. She couldn't be sure what he was saying, something about his father finding a new seed-line of heirloom carrots to plant on the family's organic farm, and Rye's sister Jordana developing a series of recipes based on the vegetables, something for a restaurant she was planning to start.

The more Rye talked, the hungrier Kat realized she was. By the time they got to the diner, she was fantasizing about home-cooked food—turkey dinner with mashed potatoes and gravy, meat loaf with peas and carrots. Rye helped her out of the truck, and he kept a protective hand beneath her elbow as he guided her into the diner, but she was already feeling much steadier on her feet.

She studied the entire menu, front to back, but ultimately, she followed Rye's lead. A bacon cheeseburger, slathered with blue cheese, thick with lettuce and juicy tomato. Fries on the side, with a single sizzling onion ring to top it all off.

Rye watched Kat tackle her meal with the single-minded determination that she devoted to everything. He'd half expected her to chicken out at the last moment, to order a side salad with a slice of lemon or some other girlie excuse for a meal.

But he had to hand it to her—she matched him bite for bite, washing down burger and fries with generous amounts of sweet tea. Maybe it was the beers that Amanda had conned her into drinking, maybe it was simple craving for a single ridiculous splurge of a meal, but Kat dug in with a gusto that astonished him.

Okay. Maybe not "astonished." He'd felt the illicit energy coiled inside her on the bench outside of Andy's. He'd felt a little of the wicked damage she could do when she let herself go unleashed.

But he'd never imagined that she would wreak so much havoc on a Smoky Blue Burger Platter. And he was damned pleased to see that she could.

"So," he said when they both finally came up for air. "The floorboards should be ready for installation next week. It'll take two days to get them down. Another day to set the ceiling tiles, and then a couple of days for painting. We'll be done in a week."

Seven days, Kat thought. Seven days, and then all the damage would be repaired. Rye would be finished at the studio, free to stay up in Richmond forever.

"Wonderful!" she said, forcing every ounce of fake cheerfulness that she could summon into the word. Oops. She must have poured it on a little *too* thick. Rye was looking at her funny. She cleared her throat. "I worked with Niffer's teacher, and I've sent home flyers with all the kids in the elementary school. We've already got two summer sessions of Beginning Ballet filled, and one of Intermediate."

"That's great! But I thought that you didn't have anyone to teach."

"Oh, I didn't tell you. I found an old recital program

in the back room on Tuesday. It was from last summer's performance, so I could still track down most of the teachers listed there. Three of them agreed to come back."

"I knew you could do it." There. That was the way enthusiasm really sounded.

Kat took another long swig of sweet tea. It was impossible to find the stuff in New York—not that she would have indulged at any point in the past ten years. Stirring artificial sweetener into iced tea didn't come anywhere close to savoring the supersaturated syrup of her childhood.

Feeling a little rebellious, she tried to imagine what her dance colleagues would say about her Eden Falls night out on the town—beer, burgers and enough sweet tea to float a luxury yacht. What did it matter, though? She couldn't remember the last time she had laughed as hard as she'd laughed with Amanda. And there were a lot worse ways to spend an evening than sitting across from a man as gorgeous as Rye Harmon.

Even if her fellow dancers would vow to eat nothing but lemon juice on iceberg lettuce for an entire week, if they had indulged like Kat.

"Hey," Rye prompted. "Are you okay?"

"I'm fine." She smiled. And she was. She was more than fine. She was relaxed and happy. "I was just thinking about what everyone is doing in New York. It's Friday night, so there's a lot of scrambling. The company does matinees on Saturday and Sunday, so everyone is probably a bit crazy."

He heard the fondness in her voice, the easy familiarity with routine. Sure, she might call them "crazy", but it was a craziness she knew and loved. "You must really miss it," he said.

"I do," she answered, but he caught the pause before she went on. As if she were looking for words. Searching for a memory. "I miss the feeling of testing myself, of pushing myself to do the most my body can do. I miss the feeling of becoming another person, someone totally different from me." She sighed. "I miss..." She trailed off, swirling an orphaned fry in ketchup.

"What, Kat?"

"Sometimes I'm not sure that I can do it." The admission seemed to unlock something in her, to free her to rush on with more words, more confessions. "The big parts, the principal dancer roles...I need to impress the company director, to prove I have what it takes. That's why I pushed myself so hard before I got hurt—extra rehearsals, extra sessions at the barre. And all I ended up with was this stupid boot and a forced month off."

He knew what she wanted him to say. He knew that she wanted to hear that she would succeed, that she would conquer her injury, that she would come back stronger than ever.

But he couldn't be certain of that. He didn't know enough about her world, about the demands of ballet life in distant New York City. No matter what *he* thought of her, how great he thought she was, he couldn't say that she had the pure strength, the unalloyed physical power to master her chosen profession's greatest challenges.

"You'll do the best that you can," he said. "And if the people who make the decisions are too foolish to take every last drop of devotion that you can give them, then you'll figure out the next step. And you'll master that. Goals, strategies and rules, right? That's what someone told me once."

She rolled her eyes. "Whoever said anything that stupid?"

"Not stupid." He shook his head. "Not stupid at all."

She flinched under the intensity of his gaze. Now that she had finished eating, the last tendrils of her tipsiness had floated away. She was sober, but her body still remembered the way that she had used it. She felt tired, raw. And with Rye staring at her that way, she felt totally exposed.

"I don't know," she said. "That stupid formula helped me when I was fourteen years old. It's probably not good for anything anymore. Not ten years later."

"It's good enough for me," Rye affirmed. "Up in Richmond this week, I applied your 'stupid formula.' I got more done in five days than I had in five weeks before that." Of course, that was the first time that he'd spent five consecutive days in his new office. The first time that he hadn't let a so-called emergency drag him back to Eden Falls.

"I'm glad I was able to help you," Kat said, trying to ignore the fact that her smile was a little wobbly around the edges.

It was funny, really. It was almost like there was a limited amount of "get up and go" to go around. Rye had listened to her, and he was moving forward with his career plan, full steam ahead. Kat, meanwhile, caught herself repeatedly musing on what life would be like if she stayed in Eden Falls.

How would it feel to teach at Morehouse Dance Academy? To stand in the center of the room, clapping out a rhythm for aspiring ballerinas, for good girls who wanted to be graceful and pretty and never, ever dance professionally on any stage, anywhere? How would it feel to stop by Susan and Mike's home every day, to watch her father continue to gain back his strength, to sit at her mother's kitchen table and drink tea using her grandmother's china? How would it feel to greet Niffer every afternoon as she got off her school bus, chattering about art projects, and reading class, and learning the capitals of all the states?

Wonderful, Kat realized, even as she was astonished to recognize that truth. Absolutely, unqualifiedly *wonderful*. In two weeks of living in Eden Falls, Kat had already had more fun than she had in the past two *years* in New York.

And what did that say about her chosen home? Her chosen career?

"Hey," Rye said, interrupting her thoughts. "Ready to get out of here?"

She nodded, sliding out of the fake leather booth. Rye paid at the cash register, waving away her attempt to reach her wallet. He held the door for her, and he ushered her into the truck, but this time she fastened her own seat belt. He smiled and stroked a single finger across her cheek before he closed the door. She shivered at the unspoken promise of that touch.

It took less time than she expected to drive to Rachel's house. Rye put the truck in Park and killed the engine. "Where's Niffer tonight?"

"Sleeping over at Mama and Daddy's. She has them wrapped around her little finger."

"Kids have a way of doing that."

She knew that it was her turn to say something, to make a joke about Niffer, about family, about something light and easy and funny. For the life of her, she couldn't imagine what she could possibly say. "Want to come in for a drink?" she finally settled on. "Of tea," she hastened to add. "Or, er, water. That's all we have inside."

"That'll be enough." Kat watched as he took the keys from the ignition, carelessly tossing them by his feet. That was yet another aspect of life in Eden Falls that she'd never see in New York. If anyone were foolish enough to own a pickup in New York, they'd keep it secured under lock and key—maybe with a mad Doberman in the cab to deter potential thieves. Somehow, it made Kat's heart sing to think of a place that was safe enough to leave car keys on the floor mat.

Inside Rachel's home, Kat headed toward the kitchen. "Let me get you a drink."

Rye caught her before she could cross the foyer, folding his hand across her flame-red scarf. "I have a confession. I'm not really thirsty."

A frisson of excitement raced across her scalp as she registered the rumble of his words. She let him turn her around, felt his other hand settle on her waist.

She was a dancer. She was used to being held by men. She was accustomed to the feeling of strong fingers on her flesh, gripping her tightly, holding her upright.

But all those sensations were her job. They were as routine, as mundane, as utterly bloodless as sitting down at a computer, typing an email, ordering supplies over the telephone.

This was something different. This was something more.

Rye felt the hitch in Kat's breath, and a lazy smile spread across his lips. He'd watched her through the evening; he knew how quickly she had sobered as she ate dinner. He had no qualms about kissing her now. Kissing. Or more.

"You know," he whispered, purposely keeping his voice so low that she had to pull closer to hear him, "we left Andy's too early tonight. We never got a chance to dance."

Her laughter was as soft as her silken hair. "In case you haven't noticed, I'm not exactly in dancing shape." She waved a hand toward her walking boot.

"I wasn't thinking of anything too strenuous. Not your pliés or arabesques or that sort of thing."

"Mmm," she whispered. "You've been doing your homework."

"All part of renovating the studio. I have to know how the space is going to be used, don't I?" That was a lie, though. He had whiled away hours in Richmond, thinking about Kat, thinking about what she did for a living. He had gone online, looking for pictures of her, and he'd picked up a bit about dance along the way.

He should have been working, of course, instead of spending his time online. Should have been focusing on Harmon Contracting. But all work and no play… He'd almost succeeded in convincing himself that his…research was good for business. That there was nothing personal in it. Nothing at all.

"Ready to sign up for a class?" she asked, obviously amused.

"I don't think either of us needs any training." He pulled her close, relishing her surprised gasp even as she yielded to his pressure. She felt marvelous in his arms, pliant but hard, melting into him even as she maintained her dancer's balance. He leaned down and found her mouth, sinking into her sweet silken heat.

Deepening the kiss, teasing her with his tongue, he raised his hand to the marble column of her throat. He could feel her pulse flutter beneath his thumb, a butterfly dancing against his flesh. His fingers wrapped around her nape, urging her closer, then skimming down the length of her spine, molding her fine-boned body to his.

He shifted his weight to match the angle of her hips, signaling his intention by an almost imperceptible tightening of his fingers against her waist. She followed his lead flawlessly, as if this were one of her fancy ballets, as if they'd practiced these moves hour after hour, night after night.

With choreography far more intimate than any Texas Two-Step, he guided her toward the couch. He half expected her to hesitate, to freeze, to refuse to follow his lead. But she sank down before he did, raising her arms above her head like some sort of exotic goddess, summoning him, asking him to join her.

Not that he required much urging.

Kat caught her breath as she lay back on the pillows of the overstuffed couch. Rye looked huge in the dim light from the foyer—sturdy and confident and *present* in a way that made her heart race. Sure, she had kissed other men. She had even fooled around on a couch or two. And practically lived with a jerk. But she had never felt this inner drive, this absolute certainty that she was doing the thing that she was meant to do, that she was with the man she was meant to be with.

For a fleeting moment, she thought of her mantra— goals, strategies, rules. There weren't any rules for the sort of passion she felt now. There wasn't any wrong or right. There was just being. Being in her own physical body. Being with Rye.

She needed to feel him, needed to know the weight of him against her.

She twined her hands around his forearm, tracing

the ropes of hard muscle, the scatter of chestnut hair. She tugged with a decisiveness that left no doubt of her intentions. "Rye," she said. "Please…"

She didn't have to ask a second time. He sank beside her, pulling her onto his lap as he sprawled against the back of the couch. She felt the rigid length of him against her thigh, the absolute confirmation that she wasn't imagining his interest, wasn't fooling herself about his need for her. Knowingly, she traced her fingernail along the denim ridge, barely restraining a grin as he groaned.

But there was more for her to explore, more of his body to know. Even as she yielded to another of his soul-rocking kisses, her fingers found the buttons of his shirt. Summoning all of her concentration, all of her determination, she undid one, and then another, and another. She tugged the tails of his shirt from his waistband and then did away with the garment altogether, tossing it onto the floor with reckless abandon.

All the while, he was doing incredible things to her neck, laving the tender spot beneath her earlobe, tangling his fingers in her hair. A crimson glow ignited in her belly as he stripped away the scarf around her hips. When he trailed the silk across her throat, drifting it over her ruby charm, the throbbing heat that rose inside her nearly made her lose her concentration, almost forced her to yield to his ministrations, to fall back against the soft couch and let him do whatever he wanted to her.

Almost.

Instead, she remembered that groan that she had incited as she traced the outline of his need. She wanted to draw that sound from him again. Relying on her taut dancer's muscles, she pulled herself upright on his lap.

She placed her hands on his shoulders, straddling his waist so that she knelt above him. For one instant, she lost her balance, pulled askew by the unaccustomed weight of her walking boot, but his hands settled beneath her rib cage, holding her, steadying her.

Before she could continue with the exploration she was determined to complete, he stripped his hands up her body, skimming off the clinging black of her top. She gasped at the sensation of cool air bathing her skin, but she was immediately warmed by the satisfaction in his gaze. While one hand spread against the small of her back, giving her the support she needed, the other flirted with the lace edge of her bra, delivering the attention she craved.

His thumb brushed against one nipple, then the other, and the sensitive buds tightened so fast that she cried out. He repeated the motion, adding a caress to the smooth plane of her belly. The red-hot fire inside her turned incandescent. She arched her back, begging him for more attention, and he lost no time complying. One hand sprang the hook on her bra, the other bared her white and willing flesh. His mouth was hot against the underside of her breasts; his tongue traced arcane patterns that left her writhing. When his lips closed over one solid pearl, she thought that she would scream. When his teeth snagged the other, she did.

Panting, eager, she forced herself to concentrate, to return to her original plan. With ragged breath, she pushed against his shoulders, making his head loll back against the couch. She left a trail of kisses along the line of his jaw, featherlight and barely hinting at all that she could do to him, for him. Her lips tingling from his rough stubble, she traced the line that had been bruised the week before, the now-invisible ache that she had given him when she had driven his pickup off the road.

She followed the logical line of that diagonal, adding her tongue to the attention of her lips. She found the dark trail of hair that marched down his tight abs, and she traced its promise, first with her lips, then with all the soft heat of her mouth, ending with the knife-edged promise of a single fingernail.

"Kat," Rye groaned when the pressure became more than he could bear. He had to feel more of her, had to find the liquid heat that spoke to his arousal. He let his palms course over her sides, felt her eager body rise to meet his. He made short work of ripping open the walking boot's straps. She sighed as he eased her foot free of the device, as he tossed the contraption to the floor. His fingers found the hidden side zipper of her crazy New York pants, and he caught his breath at the unexpected gift of lace that he revealed.

She scrambled for his waist, for the familiar bronze button of his jeans, but he caught her wrists, holding them still, bringing the fluttering birds of her fingers to rest beside her hips. There was time enough for his pleasure, time enough to find the complete release that she promised him.

He walked his fingers along the delicate top of her panties, measuring the taut tremble of her belly. She followed his silent command, raising her hips to meet him, to beg him, to invite him to share in the glory that she promised. With the lightest of touches, he traced the hollow behind her right knee, the sensitive cave carved by her tendons. She bucked against the sensation, and he caught a laugh in the back of his throat.

Kat moaned his name, reaching up to pull him down on top of her. She needed to feel his weight against her, needed him to anchor her. Something about the gesture, though, brought full realization crashing down upon her. She'd had no intention of bringing a man back to Rachel's home. She'd had no plan to make love that night.

She had no protection.

"Rye," she whispered, hating every word she had to say. "I don't have...anything. We can't..."

"Hush," he said, and the fingers that he traced along her inner thigh nearly sent her over some crazed edge. "We won't."

Before she could flounder in the sea of disappointment that his words released upon her, his fingers went back to the lace edge of her panties, to the damp panel of silk beneath. "Rye —" she protested.

"Hush," he whispered again, but now he breathed the word against the most secret part of her, turning it into a promise. She closed her eyes as his fingers slipped beneath the lace; she caught her breath as his thumb found the pearl between her legs. One gentle flick, two and she was writhing for release.

He laughed again, ripping away the last of the lacy barrier. She felt his stubble against her thighs, gently raking one leg and then the other. Forgetting her dancer's control, she tilted her hips, longing for the ultimate pleasure that she knew he was prepared to give her.

A single velvet stroke of his tongue. Another. One last, savoring caress, and then she was crashing over a precipice, clutching at his hair, tumbling down an endless slope of clenching, throbbing pleasure.

Rye watched the storm pass over her body, the beautiful twist of her lips as she breathed his name, over and over and over again. When it was past, when he knew that she was drifting on a formless, shapeless sea of comfort, he eased himself up her body. She was utterly relaxed as he pulled her languid form to lie on top of him. Her hair spread across his chest, and the warmth of her flushed cheek soothed his own pounding heart.

"Mmm," she murmured, and her fingers drifted down his torso.

"Rest," he said, smoothing one hand down the plane of her back, while the other cupped the curve of her neck.

"I want…" she whispered, but she drifted into silence before she finished the sentence.

He eased himself to a more comfortable position, telling himself that his body's demands would quiet in a few minutes, that the ache below his belt would ease. He underestimated, though, the force of the woman whom he cradled. He had not considered the power of her honey-apricot scent, teasing him with every breath he drew. He had not taken into account her soft pressure against his chest, his thighs, his entire excruciatingly primed body.

But he managed to take comfort in Kat's utter peacefulness as her breathing slowed. He waited, and he watched, and he held her until she slipped into the deepest of sleeps.

Only then did he look around the living room, seeing the home that Rachel had let fall into disrepair. He could fix things up in short order. Rip out the awful carpet, put down a new floor. Replace the fogged storm windows with something that would insulate the house better. Renovate the entire kitchen, with its creaky old appliances.

It wouldn't take long. A couple of weeks. A month. He could stay in Eden Falls while he worked, keep an eye on every step of the process.

No.

He wasn't going to stay in Eden Falls. He lived in Richmond now. He had a life for himself, a business that he had fought hard for. For the first time in his adult life, he was free to do what he wanted to do, free from family and clinging girlfriends.

Kat shifted in her sleep, spreading her hand across his chest.

What the hell was he doing here? Maybe he had come home with Kat precisely because he knew that *she* wasn't sticking around Eden Falls. She had been absolutely clear—she was heading back to New York, just as soon as he could finish work on the studio. She was safe. She wasn't going to take over his life. She wasn't going to be another Marissa, teasing him, shaping his life to hers, then leaving him in her dust.

Kat had already built a life for herself, a life outside of Eden Falls. She had remained true to herself, true to the promises she'd made when she was just a kid.

Was he really such a wimp that he couldn't do the same? He had *vowed* that he would make a go of things in Richmond. Moving away was what he'd always wanted, what he needed, to prove that he was a real man.

He couldn't give all that away. Not for an impossible future. Not for an unknown, unmeasured relationship with Kat, who had already found her own path to independence.

A chill settled over the room as the final heat of their exertion faded. Rye fought against a shudder, forcing himself to stay perfectly still, lest he ruin Kat's sleep. The night grew long, and he watched and waited and thought about all the futures that might be, and one that he would never, ever have.

Chapter Six

Rye stood in the dance studio, surveying the stack of hardwood flooring. Brandon was the cousin he'd enlisted for assistance that day. He was pretty sure the guy had only agreed to come over because he hoped Amanda Morehouse would be visiting Kat. Rye had probably implied as much, now that he thought about it. He didn't feel too guilty, though. In the past, Brandon had roped Rye into worse duty on the family's huge organic farm.

"The staple guns are out in the truck," Rye said. "The saw is there, too, along with the rolls of waterproofing to lay out beneath the wood."

"I'm pretty sure that I'm the one who taught *you* how to install a hardwood floor," Brandon retorted.

"Just trying to be helpful," Rye said. He didn't mind his cousin's gruff reply. Instead, he took advantage of

Brandon's expertise to head toward the office, to the private refuge where he knew Kat was hard at work.

Kat. Even now, he could feel her weight on his chest, her body melted and cooling after the pleasure he had given her. The memory, though, made a corner of his heart curl in reflexive avoidance.

He hadn't thought this through. He hadn't realized quite how hard he was falling for Kat, how much she had come to mean to him. There was no way that their lives could ever come together—she was determined to get back to New York the second she was shed of that walking boot, if not before. It had been what? Three weeks already? She'd said that she was only going to wear it for a month. One more week—at most—and then she'd be gone forever.

And he certainly couldn't put all the blame on her for his current discomfort. He hadn't been lying when he'd told her he had an early Saturday meeting in Richmond. Late Friday night, actually early Saturday morning, he had finally carried her to her bed, tucked her in beneath her comforter and stroked her hair until she fell back to sleep. But then he'd left, hitting the road, letting the freeway roll out beneath his headlights as he drove home in the dark of night.

He hadn't called on Saturday. Sunday either. He'd needed to put some distance between them—emotional space to match the physical one.

This whole thing shouldn't be as difficult as it was turning out to be. So what if Kat was heading back to New York soon? Rye could always come down to Eden Falls, stay here until she left. Who knew what would grow between them in the time that they had?

No.

He wasn't going to do that again. Wasn't going to

cash in his dreams. If he walked away from Richmond now, he knew that he would never again find the nerve to build his own business. He would stay here in Eden Falls until he was old and withered and gray, until he couldn't even remember what to do with a woman as intoxicating as Kat.

Damn.

He knocked lightly on the door frame. "Mornin'," he said as Kat looked up from behind the desk.

God, she was beautiful. Her hair was back in one of those twists off her neck, making her look like every schoolboy's fantasy librarian. Her silvery eyes brightened when she saw him, and her smile made his heart ache.

"I missed you," she said. "It was a long weekend without you."

He was supposed to apologize for living in his new hometown. He couldn't. No. He *wouldn't*. Instead, he asked, "What did you do?"

"Niffer had a T-ball game. You didn't tell me that you're a million times better coach than Noah is."

He shrugged, fighting against the pang that told him he should have been there for the game. "Britney was out of town, so Noah didn't have an excuse not to be there."

Kat laughed. "Daddy was feeling so much better that Mama let him walk down to the park with us. We had to take it slow, but he made it. It was great to see him out of the house, soaking up the sunshine."

"That's good news." He felt stiff as he said the words. Awkward. This was terrible—he felt like he was lying to Kat with every word he said. Every word he didn't.

"How was Richmond?" she asked, the faintest hint of worry etching a thin line between her brows.

He forced himself to answer with a hearty smile. "Everything is going great. That Saturday morning meeting was with a new client—a massive kitchen renovation. Yesterday, I met with a computer guy—he's set up all my client files."

Kat wasn't an idiot. She could tell that something was wrong.

Something. There wasn't a lot of mystery about that, was there? What was the one thing that had changed since she and Rye had last talked, had been easy and comfortable and happy in each other's company? Her cheeks grew hot, and she wasn't sure whether the leap in her pulse was because of the memories of what they had done, or her regrets about what they hadn't.

But that wasn't all. She understood the warning behind Rye's stilted conversation. She *knew* that he lived in Richmond now, that he was only here in Eden Falls as a favor to her. He didn't even *want* to be working on the studio. That was just as well. She was going back to New York, after all, leaving all of this behind in just a matter of days.

And that thought left her strangely numb, as it had every time she thought it over the weekend.

But that was ridiculous. New York was her home, had been for ten years. New York was the place where she had her friends, her job, her life.

She thought of the gray concrete canyons, the buildings so tall that sunshine never touched the streets. Before she could be depressed by the memory of such a bleak landscape, though, she forced herself to confront the hard facts of living in Eden Falls. A big night out was stopping by the cinema to watch a first-release film. There wasn't a single twenty-four-hour business in town. The only restaurants that made deliveries were the pizza parlor on Elm Street and the Chinese place on Baker.

But she and Amanda had had a lot of fun at the movies, just last night. She'd left Niffer with her parents, and she and her cousin had shared a huge tub of popcorn, watched some silly chick-flick. After all, who needed to work twenty-four hours a day? And why would she ever need to order in anything other than pizza or Chinese?

No. She could never live in Eden Falls long-term. No matter how much fun she was having on this spring break. Vacation wasn't the real world, even a vacation rooted in caring for her healing father, for her wayward niece.

Bottom line—it was absolutely, positively 100% necessary to drive around a town like Eden Falls. Kat had been imposing on her mother and Amanda for the entire time she'd been here. Sooner or later, her family was going to refuse to ferry her from one place to another. And she had no intention of making another disastrous attempt at getting behind the wheel.

Eden Falls had nothing on New York. She just had to remember that.

In fact, there was one more dangerous thing about Eden Falls: Rye Harmon. She had a sudden vision of his lips on the inside of her thigh. Her cheeks flushed at the memory of the pleasure he had given her. At the thought of the fulfillment he'd denied himself. She had to say something, had to let him know that she had stopped by Doherty's Drugstore the day before. He needed to know that she had purchased a packet of silver-wrapped condoms, to use in the future.

Whatever future they had. She cleared her throat. "Rye, about Friday night," she began, even though she had no earthly idea what she was going to say after that.

He answered her quickly, too quickly. "I shouldn't have… I'm sorry. I live in Richmond now. I —"

"Rye!" She cut him off, touched by how flustered he'd become. "I know that. I understand."

"It's just that in the past… There was someone who…" He ran his fingers through his hair, leaving his chestnut curls in disarray. "I'm making a total mess out of this."

She caught his hands and pulled them close to her chest. "No," she said, meeting his eyes. "You're not. I'm not expecting you to drop everything and move back here to Eden Falls. I'd be crazy to ask that, when I'm only here for a while myself. Friday night was amazing—and I hope we'll spend more time together before I go back to New York. But I'm not expecting you to walk in here with an engagement ring and the keys to your family's Eden Falls house."

Right then, for just that moment, when her smile got a little crooked and she squeezed his fingers between her own, he would have left Richmond. He would have dropped Harmon Contracting, abandoned all his hopes and dreams.

But then he heard Brandon shift equipment out in the studio. It was like his cousin was trying to remind him of his business, of his future, of all the reasons he'd fought to get out of Eden Falls.

Rye was an independent businessman now. And Kat wasn't part of his past. She wasn't Marissa Turner. She was a woman who had found her way clear of Eden Falls years before. That was part of what made her so damned alluring.

He slipped his fingers free from her gentle grip, but he stepped even closer. His palm cupped the back of her neck, and he leaned down to steal a quick kiss. She was more hesitant than he'd expected, though, almost as if she were afraid of the spark that might ignite between them.

Well, spark be damned. His free hand settled on the small of her back, tugging her closer, so that he could feel the whole long line of her body. He traced her closed lips with his tongue, and his blood leaped high when she yielded to him. Before he could follow through, though, before he could think about easing up the rumpled cloth of her blouse, there was another clatter from the outer room.

"That's Brandon," he breathed, settling his forehead on Kat's shoulder and drawing a steadying breath. "He's ready to install the floorboards."

Kat's own breath hitched as she took a step back. What was she thinking, anyway? She wasn't exactly the type of girl to revel in a little afternoon delight—not with countless business details left to take care of.

"Great," she said, trying not to sound too rueful. Then, she repeated the word, broadcasting it for Brandon's hearing. "Great! Let me show you this website that I found. I can use it to design stationery for the studio—letterhead and flyers and business cards."

He edged around the desk, coming to stand behind her as she pulled her chair closer to the computer. She sat like a classical statue, straight and tall. Her hands flew over her computer keyboard, smoothly competent as she called up something on the screen. He didn't care about any stupid website. He was just pleased for the excuse to be standing so close to her.

"Look at this," she enthused. "They have hundreds

of templates—you can choose one that's right for you. Here, I'll show you. Let's make a flyer for Harmon Contracting. Didn't you say that you needed to do that?"

She looked at him expectantly, and he nodded, eager to see her smile. He wasn't disappointed.

"They have themes, like Medicine and Legal." She let the computer mouse hover over those choices for a moment to illustrate the possibilities, and then she swept it toward the top of the screen. "But we probably want Carpentry."

She clicked once, and the screen was filled with the image of a creamy white page. Silvery scrolls curled around the edges, folding into twined hearts in the corners. Ornate writing spelled out the formal words of an invitation: Mr. and Mrs. Robert Smith request the pleasure of your presence at the wedding of their daughter...

"Oops!" Kat slammed her palm down on the mouse, as if it were a living creature that might actually scurry away. "I clicked on Celebrations by mistake."

He couldn't help himself. He grinned at her obvious discomfort. She was acting like that one false click was a much bigger deal than it was. From her level of embarrassment, it was almost like she'd unveiled some deep dark secret, as if he had walked in on her while she was showering.

He felt the first stirring of his body responding to that delightful image, and he shifted his weight from one foot to the other. *Business, Harmon*, he remonstrated with himself. This was a business website that she was showing him.

By the time he had schooled his mind back to professionalism, she had brought up a different page. Hearts had been replaced with tiny images of a hammer and saw in one corner, a toolbox in another. Bold lettering stated John Smith Handyman Services, with a mock address at 123 Main Street.

"See?" Kat said, and she was studying the computer screen just a little too intensely, staring at the page as if it might turn into a bird and take flight. "I can click here, and we can change the name." He watched as her fingers picked out "Harmon Contracting." "We can add your Richmond address. There's room for an email address, a landline, and your cell phone. You can keep the dark brown, or you can make it any other color. Navy, maybe. Or maroon."

"What if I want the silver, from the other screen?"

He couldn't say what made him ask the question. It wasn't fair, really. He just wanted to see emotion skip across her features, flash across her platinum eyes. She darted a glance toward the office door, toward the studio where Brandon served as unwitting chaperone.

Kat cleared her throat, consciously deciding not to take the bait. Instead, she dashed her fingers across the keyboard, pulling up the draft files she had created for her own business, for the dance studio. Toe shoes filled the corners, and the lettering was a professional burgundy. Morehouse Dance Academy. The street address. Eden Falls, Virginia.

She had completed the flyer with information about all of the classes that they offered, from Introductory Ballet to Advanced Showcase. Instructors' names were listed inside parentheses—Miss Sarah, Miss Emma, Miss Virginia. The only blank class was the Advanced Showcase; the former teacher had not responded to the dozen messages Kat had left.

That made sense, actually. Miss Courtney Thomson had been the most accomplished of the studio's instructors. She was likely to take her career the most seriously, to have been the most turned off by Rachel's haphazard management. Kat suspected that she'd already taken on work in a neighboring town, moved on with her life. Kat really couldn't blame her.

"That's great," Rye said, and she realized that he'd been reading the full text on the page.

"It's nothing," she said, but she was pleased by the compliment. She'd spent a lot of time on Saturday writing the brochure. "I need to take it to my mother this afternoon."

"She'll love it. It reads like something from a professional advertising company."

"We can do something similar for you. Specific to plumbing and electricity and stuff."

"Stuff," he teased. "You make it sound so complicated."

"You know what I mean!"

"Yeah, I do," he admitted. Without fully intending to, he placed his hands on the back of her chair, spinning her around to face him. He heard her breath catch in her throat as he edged forward. She looked up at him, an uncertain smile quirking her lips. He leaned down and planted his palms on the arms of her chair, the motion bringing his lips close to hers. "I know exactly what you mean," he growled, and suddenly neither of them was talking about stationery or computers or… stuff.

Before he could follow through on the promise of the suddenly charged air between them, a clatter came from the studio. Something metal hit the floor, followed by a sharp curse.

"Brandon?" Rye called, already turning to the door.

"I'm all right," came the quick reply. "But I could use a hand out here."

Rye set his hand against Kat's cheek. "I—" he said, so softly that Brandon could never hear him. He wasn't sure what he was going to say. *I want to finish what we started Friday night. I don't care about stationery, not when we could be talking about something else. Doing something else. I don't give a damn about Richmond, or New York, or Eden Falls, or anyplace, so long as I'm with you.*

"Go," Kat said, and she watched him swallow hard. "I'll be here. Brandon needs you."

She slumped into her chair as he hurried out the door. She should have Rye check the air-conditioning in the office. It was about twenty degrees too hot in the small room. She pretended not to hear the muffled curses as the men negotiated over some spilled hardware.

Before Kat could pull herself together enough to go back to the stationery website, the computer chimed. She had new email. She clicked on the icon, opening up a message entitled Coppelia. The sender was Haley, writing from New York.

The first paragraph was a breathless apology for failing to write more often. Haley's on-again, off-again boyfriend was back in her life; he'd given her red roses for her birthday—*two dozen!!!* The apartment was fine. Slimeball Adam had finally come and picked up his junk. Skanky Selene had already dumped him and moved on to another dancer in the company. Kat's eyes skimmed over the words, as if she were reading some boring nineteenth-century novel about people she'd never met.

But then she saw the real reason for Haley's message.

Sign up for *Coppelia* auditions closes at midnight, May 1. You have to do it in person; they won't let me add your name to the list. Are you coming back in time?

Kat stared at the screen, at the Xes and Os that closed out Haley's message. *Are you coming back in time?*

Coppelia. Kat had always dreamed of dancing the lead role of Swanilda. The ballet had been her absolute favorite, ever since she was a little girl. It told the story of a lonely toymaker in a mountain village, a mad scientist who created a life-size doll who only needed the sacrifice of a human being to come to life. Swanilda was the wise village girl who figured out the madness of the toymaker's work—she saved her betrothed from being sacrificed. Swanilda defeated the mad wood-carver and married her beloved.

The role was physically demanding. In addition to classical ballet moves, the part required executing a number of country dances and one extended section where Swanilda pretended to be the jerky windup doll, Coppelia.

Kat flexed her toes inside her walking boot. Even when she arched them to their full reach, she felt nothing, no twinge of pain. Her foot was almost healed.

She looked around the office. Despite her still-elevated heart rate as she listened for Rye, out in the studio, her work here was nearly done. She could place her order for stationery right now. That would leave one last thing to clean up: the bank accounts. Kat couldn't believe that she'd let the problem linger for nearly three full weeks. But it wasn't really a surprise. The lost money was the one thing she couldn't fix. That was Rachel's one failing that Kat couldn't tidy up, couldn't erase away. Her parents would be devastated, and there was nothing Kat could do—and so she'd let herself shrug off the responsibility, ever since she'd identified the problem.

But for the past week or so, there had been another reason that she'd failed to handle the financial crisis. Once she told her mother about the lost money, there'd be no reason left to stay in Eden Falls. And Kat had to admit that part of her did not want to leave.

That was only natural, she tried to assure herself. Her father had looked so healthy as he walked to the park on Sunday. He was sitting up in his recliner at home, even heading to the kitchen to get his own snacks. Susan would be able to run the studio on her own soon enough; Amanda could probably juggle her own teaching schedule to help out for the first rough weeks of transition.

Even Niffer had calmed down. Sure, the child still whined when she didn't get her way. And she would choose candy over a healthy meal, given half a chance. But she'd taken to the new structure in her life like the duck to water. Just that morning, she had returned her crayons to her toy box without being asked to straighten up the kitchen table.

For all intents and purposes, Kat's work here was done. Except for the accounting ledger.

Out in the studio, Rye laughed at something Brandon said. No. Rye was not a reason to stay in Eden Falls. He lived in Richmond. He was on the threshold of his own successful career.

She flashed again on a memory of how incredible it had felt to lie within the shelter of his arms. His heartbeat had pounded against her own. His warmth had enfolded her as she drifted off to sleep.

She had braved the embarrassment of shopping at the drugstore, of securing the protection they needed, so that they could complete what they'd started Friday night.

No. Rye was a spring fling. A light touch of relief as she juggled all the responsibilities of family. An enjoyable confirmation that her demanding life in New York hadn't ruined her, that she could still be a desirable woman.

She didn't have any right to turn their fun and games into anything more. It wouldn't be fair to Rye. It wouldn't be fair to herself.

Squaring her shoulders, Kat clicked on the button to reply to Haley's email. She typed:

Glad to hear all is well. I'm wrapping things up here and should be home in time to sign up. Thanks a million times over! XOXO. Kat

She read the message four times before she clicked Send. And then she dug out the studio's oversize checkbook, determined to calculate all of Rachel's red ink, down to the last penny. Then, she'd be free to leave Eden Falls. To return to her home. To New York.

Out in the studio, Rye was pleased to find that a drop cloth had caught the spilled staples and oversize staple gun that Brandon had dropped. Nevertheless, he said to his cousin, "Let's take this thing outside. I don't want anything to scratch the new floorboards."

"You're the boss," Brandon said. He hitched up his Levi's before he helped Rye maneuver the heavy cloth out the door.

It was only when they stood in the parking lot that

Rye said, "Wait a second. There's just a handful of staples." He looked over at Brandon. "What the hell made so much noise?"

"You mean this?" Brandon reached into the bed of the truck, fishing out a clean metal tray for painting. He shoved it beneath the tarp and then emptied a box of staples onto it. The clatter was suitably dramatic.

"What the—"

"I had to get you out of that office, buddy."

"What are you talking about?"

"I heard the two of you talking. Don't you realize that girl thinks you're picking out wedding invitations?"

Rye laughed. "You don't know what you're talking about. She accidentally pulled up that screen. She was showing me how to put together flyers for the new business."

Brandon snorted. "You've got it bad, don't you? You'll believe just about anything."

"You couldn't see the computer screen, Bran. I'm telling you, it was filled with ballet shoes."

"What if I want the silver, from the other screen?" Brandon quoted.

Rye sighed. "I was just teasing her. There isn't anything serious between us. There can't be. She's heading back to New York in a week or two."

Brandon bent to retrieve the paint tray and staples, taking his time to stow them in the bed of the pickup. He was still facing the truck when he muttered, "That shouldn't be the only reason there isn't anything serious."

Of course, Rye heard him. Rye was pretty sure he was *supposed* to hear him. "What are you talking about?"

"Hey, I've got eyes. And I know you. I knew you a

couple of years ago, when that crazy Marissa chick was jerking you around, and you were practically living on my couch."

"I wasn't living on your couch."

Brandon pinned him with glittering eyes. "No, you just stopped by every other night because I'm such a wonderful cook. Come on, man. That was Johnnie Walker *Gold* that we killed the night your Marissa said she was heading out to California."

"She wasn't 'my' Marissa," Rye said automatically.

"Of course not. She was just the reason you forfeited the lease on your first place up in Richmond. And put off getting your contractor's license, for two years running. And didn't bid on that antebellum mansion gig. Or that showcase house. Or—"

"Okay!" Rye clenched his fists, his stomach churning at the memory of all the opportunities he'd let go because of Marissa.

"No," Brandon said. "It's not okay. Because I see you doing the same thing, all over again. You're throwing away your life, because of a woman. You're staying in Eden Falls, even after you promised to get the hell out of Dodge."

"I have an office up in Richmond, Bran." Rye barely held his temper in check.

"And just look at how much time you're spending up there." Brandon reached into the back of the truck, pulling a soda out of the cooler that was lashed to the bed. He popped the top and passed it to Rye before salvaging another for himself. He downed half the drink in a few noisy swallows before gesturing with the can. "Don't do this, buddy. I'm telling you. She isn't worth it."

She's worth a lot more than you know, Rye thought.

You haven't seen her, the way she can laugh. The way she cares about—really loves—her niece. The way she's set aside her own life, helping out her family when they need her. You haven't seen the way she looks with her hair down, and her lips swollen from a good kiss, and....

But of course he didn't say anything out loud. Instead, he sipped from his own soft drink can and stared across the parking lot, as if the billboard on the far side held the answer to all the secrets of the universe.

He wasn't going to fight his cousin over this. Especially when he knew that Brandon was right about one thing. Kat was going to leave Eden Falls, and then all the fun and games would be over. Kat was heading back to the National Ballet and New York, to the life that she'd built for herself.

And nothing Rye could say would change that. Marissa Turner had taught him that, for sure. He could never control a woman. Only himself. Only his own decisions.

Brandon finished his soda in another long swig, belching before he crushed the can and tossed it into the back of the truck. "I pity you, buddy. You've sure got it bad."

Rye punched him on the shoulder. "Shut up, Bran, okay? Let's get back in there. It's time to get this job done."

"You're the boss. Just remember, you can hang out on my couch, anytime you need to."

As Brandon headed back into the studio, Rye pretended to remember that he had to make a phone call. He was only standing there, though, with his mobile beside his ear. Standing there and realizing that Brandon was right. Rye did have it bad.

Because no matter how this ended, no matter how broken up he would be when Kat went back to New York, he wasn't ready to stop yet. No, this wasn't the same as it had been with Marissa. He wasn't going to throw his own life away, just because of a woman.

But he was going to enjoy himself while he could. He was going to follow through on the unspoken offer that Kat had made when she invited him in for a drink. He was going to enjoy whatever time they had together— a week, two weeks, whatever.

He just had to make sure things didn't get messy. He just had to make sure that neither of them expected more than the other was offering. He just had to make sure that there were no strings attached.

Picking out wedding invitations. Brandon didn't know what the hell he was talking about. Kat wasn't some flighty girl, living her entire life with the single goal of getting a wedding band on her finger. She'd be just as happy as Rye was to enjoy whatever they had, for however long they had it. And when it came time to put her on the Yankee Clipper and send her back north, that was exactly what he would do.

After a few minutes, Rye realized that he must look like an idiot, standing in a parking lot, holding a cell phone to his ear, not saying a word. As he slid his phone back into his pocket, he realized that he felt like an idiot, too. He could bluster and boast all he wanted, but there was a truth he had to admit—at least to himself.

He had fallen for Kat Morehouse. Fallen hard. And no amount of saying otherwise would change the shape of the hole she was going to leave in his heart when she headed back to New York City.

Chapter Seven

Kat watched proudly as Niffer ate the last bite of broccoli on her plate. "Thank you for dinner, Gram," the little girl said. "It was almost as good as dinner last night."

Well, so much for perfect manners, Kat thought. At least Susan was smiling at Niffer indulgently. "And what did you girls do for dinner last night?"

Niffer answered before Kat could. "Mr. Harmon took us out for tacos!"

"Oh, really?" Susan arched a smile toward Kat before darting a look at Mike. Kat's father made a show of chewing his meat loaf.

"We just grabbed something quick, Mama. Sort of a celebration for getting the painting done at the studio." Kat heard the way her voice rose in pitch, even though she tried to sound casual. There was just a shadow of a hint of a possibility of a chance that Susan would accept the fact that Rye had treated them to a casual Mexican dinner for no reason whatsoever.

The questions would never stop coming, though, if Kat gave any hint of the midday break she had taken Wednesday afternoon....

It had all started innocently enough. Rye had said that she should leave the office for the rest of the day, that the paint fumes would get too strong. He had driven her home, confirming that Niffer was well-occupied with her after-school program. And then, he had ushered Kat into her bedroom, barely taking time to close the door behind him. They had both laughed as they produced identical silver-wrapped packets from behind the counter at Doherty's.

No. Susan didn't need to know anything at all about that. If Kat had had *her* way, her mother wouldn't have known anything about the taco dinner the night before, either.

Completely innocent, Niffer wiped her mouth with her napkin before folding the cloth and putting it beside her plate. "May I be excused, Gram?"

Susan looked astonished by the polite request, but she nodded at the little girl. "Certainly, Jen—um, Niffer. Thank you for asking so nicely."

Kat helped her niece wriggle down from the dining room chair. When she turned back to the table, Susan was shaking her head in amazement. "You have worked wonders with her, sweetheart."

Kat lifted her chin and smiled. "I really think she wanted some structure in her life. You always said that you and Daddy set your rules so that Rachel and I would know how much you love us."

Mike looked up from his armchair at the head of the

table. "I didn't think you listened to a word your mother and I said while you were growing up."

"Daddy!" Kat laughed. "Of course I did. I can recite all your lessons by heart." She closed her eyes and raised up a finger, as if she were recounting the Ten Commandments. "A fool and his money are soon parted." She added a second finger. "If you don't have anything nice to say, don't say anything at all." One more finger. "Never assume malice, when stupidity is an explanation."

Susan laughed. "She has you there, love. I think the only thing she learned from me is 'stop making that face, or it might freeze that way.'"

Kat shook her head. "No, Mama. You taught us a lot more than that." Before she could elaborate, though, the phone rang.

Susan bustled into the kitchen, only to return with the handset. "What? I can't hear you! There's too much noise in the background!" Susan took the phone away from her ear and squinted at the buttons. She punched the one for volume five times in rapid succession. "Who is this?" she shouted back into the phone.

"Mom!" Now the sound was loud enough that Kat could make out her sister's voice.

"Rachel?" Susan looked as if she might drop the phone. Kat heard a skitter of footsteps, and Niffer was back in the room, hugging her grandmother and reaching for the handset as if it were a lifeline. Susan pulled back a little before she shouted, "Where are you?"

"I'm in D.C., Mom! Staying with friends! We're having a party!"

Mike muttered at the far end of the table, "Tell me something I don't know."

Niffer started whining, "Mommy! Let me talk to Mommy!"

Susan shushed her granddaughter. "Rachel, when are you coming home?"

"That's why I called, Mom!"

Niffer was still whimpering, trying to get her little hands on the phone. "Hush," Kat said. "Come here, Niffer. You can sit on my lap, and we'll talk to Mommy after Gram is done." She measured out the moment when the little girl thought about refusing, but then Niffer let herself be held.

Rachel was still shouting over the line. "I'm catching a ride tomorrow! I'll be there by noon!"

"Wonderful, dear," Susan said. "Niffer has a T-ball game tomorrow afternoon. You can see her play."

"Who?"

"Niffer. Jenny."

There was a commotion on the other end of the line, some sort of shouting match that resolved into a cluster of voices shouting "Ten! Nine! Eight!"

Rachel added her own treble above the countdown. "Gotta go, Mom! See you tomorrow!"

The silence in the room echoed after the connection was broken. Susan stared at the handset as if it might come back to life. Mike scowled, his thoughts about his wayward daughter patently clear on his face. Kat shook her head. Rachel hadn't mentioned her at all, hadn't even asked about their father's health.

Niffer, though, bounced off Kat's lap and ran across the room to hug Susan. "Mommy's coming home! I get to see Mommy tomorrow!"

Susan smoothed her granddaughter's hair. "Yes, dear," she said automatically.

Kat sat back in her chair. Looking at her parents'

faces, she realized that Susan and Mike thought the same thing she did. Rachel was about as likely to show up at Niffer's T-ball game as she was to win a Nobel Prize. The interstate to D.C. might as well have been the Trans-Continental Railroad. And there was no real way to cushion the blow for an excited little girl.

Kat had to do something, though. "Niffer, honey. Go pick up your toys in the other room. Gram is going to drive us home in five minutes."

When Niffer looked up, a spark of her old rebellion glinted deep in her coal-black eyes. "When Mommy's back, Gram won't have to drive us everywhere. Mommy's smart enough to drive a car."

"Niffer!" Susan warned.

Kat, though, waved off the confrontation. "Clean up your toys, Niffer. Now."

The little girl dragged her feet as she harrumphed across the room.

Mike glared after her. "I thought that child was through with all her back-talking."

Kat shrugged. "She's just excited. And I don't have the heart to get angry with her, because I know she's going to end up disappointed tomorrow."

"You don't *know* that," Susan tsked.

Kat sighed. "I hope you're right, Mama."

No one said another word on the topic. But Kat couldn't help but realize her father didn't correct her. He was as mistrustful of Rachel as she was. It was a long ride home, listening to Niffer ramble on about all the presents she hoped her mother would bring.

Rye glanced in the mirror of the hotel lobby, making sure that his tie was straight before he went into the conference room. He could already hear the murmur of conversation inside, the movers and shakers of the Richmond business world conducting their most important deals at the monthly Chamber of Commerce dinner. He was willing to bet that the salads had already been served, that the bone-dry breasts of chicken were on their way.

He'd rather be in Eden Falls. He'd rather be sitting in Susan and Mike Morehouse's dining room, watching Niffer wrinkle up her nose at the broccoli that she had already denounced when he took her out for tacos the night before. He'd made Niffer promise to eat every last bite, saying that her grandmother would be disappointed if she left any vegetables on her plate.

Kat's smile had been blinding. Or maybe he'd just been blinded by memories of Wednesday afternoon. Everything had seemed so simple when he had taken her home from the studio, using the paint fumes as an excuse for playing hooky. So easy. So *right*. Even now, he could hear her laughing as she told him some story about Niffer. He could hardly believe that he had ever thought of Kat as icy. As cold. As utterly, completely controlled in everything she did. He couldn't wait to see her lose that firm control again. As soon as he could get back down to Eden Falls.

"Hey, Rye!"

"Josh!" Rye extended his hand toward his fraternity brother. "I wasn't expecting to see you here."

"This is where the big deals get done, right?" Josh Barton flashed his old winning smile. "I heard a rumor you had set up shop here in Richmond."

"I figured it was finally time to get out of Eden Falls."

"Past time, I'd imagine." Josh had always been restless, even back in college. Rye supposed that was part of his charm with the ladies—the man dreamed big, and he wasn't afraid to have company on his journey. "What sort of work are you doing these days?"

Rye felt himself relax in the face of Josh's easy confidence. "A couple of kitchens, lately. Last winter, I did a complete restore on the old Wilson place. And just this week I finished renovating the Morehouse Dance Studio."

"*That* must have been a pain. Is that crazy Rachel still running the place for her mother?"

"Not for a while. She took off to visit friends out west." Rye shrugged. His explanation sounded better than, *she left town, ditching your daughter with her parents.* "Her sister came down from New York to help out. Kat."

"She's the one who went to that fancy ballet school?"

Rye nodded. He didn't want to talk to Josh about Kat. In fact, now that he thought about it, it was strange that Josh hadn't been around to help with Niffer. Take her for a weekend, at least. Especially since the guy still seemed to be pretty tied in to Eden Falls life. He'd asked about Rachel running the studio. He had to know about Mike Morehouse's illness, about the way the community was rallying to help out the family.

"At least one of those girls turned out sane." Josh gave Rye a knowing wink.

"What do you mean?"

"Come on! You know as well as I do—Rachel is *nuts!*"

No matter how much Rye might have agreed, the blatant criticism raised his chivalrous hackles. "She was always a little wild, yeah, but I wouldn't call her 'nuts.'"

Josh grinned. "Are we talking about the same woman? Played the field after she got out of high school? Spent half her time at the frat house, then tried to frame me for eighteen years of child support?"

A sliver of warning slipped into Josh's tone. "Frame?"

Josh shook his head. "That crazy bitch sued me for paternity. She had to withdraw the case, though, after all the tests came back. I dodged a bullet with that one!"

Rye laughed, because that's what he was supposed to do. Even as he responded on automatic pilot, though, his jaw was tightening into a stony line.

Josh shot his cuffs and nodded toward the conference room. "But enough about Eden Falls. You're in Richmond now. Ready to meet your new business partners?"

"You go ahead," Rye said. "I'm going to make a pit stop."

Rye watched in dismay as Josh disappeared down the hall. His ears were ringing, as if the lobby echoed. A metallic taste coated the back of his throat. *Dodged a bullet.*

Rachel Morehouse had told Rye, in no uncertain terms, that Josh Barton was the father of her baby. Rachel had said that her baby would never have a handyman for a father; no one but a lawyer was good enough for Rachel. Rachel had said that Rye was off the hook. Rachel had said...

Rye clutched at the marble counter in front of the mirror. Closing his eyes, he could see Niffer's jet-black hair, a perfect match for her mother's. But he could see the line of her jaw, as well, a line echoed in a dozen of Rye's nieces and nephews. And he could picture the girl standing at the plate in T-ball, getting ready to swing the bat left-handed. Rye looked down at his own left hand, staring at his palm as if he'd never seen it before.

For whatever twisted reason that passed as logic in

Rachel's rebellious mind, she had lied to him five years ago. Jennifer Morehouse was Rye's daughter.

Kat made sure that her father was comfortably settled on one of the benches behind home plate, and then she nodded toward a vendor who had set up his cart on the edge of the park. "Can I get you a hot dog, Daddy?"

"No, thanks. I'm fine."

"A Coke, then?"

"I don't need anything."

Susan had been worried about the late-afternoon start of the game; she hadn't wanted anyone to go hungry. As a result, she'd spent the afternoon setting out "nibbles"—cheese and crackers and fruit and cookies—three times as much food as any normal meal. Kat didn't think she'd ever be hungry again.

As much as she was inclined to fuss over her father, she had to admit that he *did* look strong. Sure, his shirt hung loose at his throat. And his tight-belted trousers rode a little high on his hips. But the fresh air had brought color to his cheeks. He'd made the walk from the house without getting winded, in his best time yet since his surgery. Kat sat down beside him, but barely a minute passed before she jumped up and looked over her shoulder.

Mike's mouth pursed into a frown. "Don't waste your time looking for her, Kat. You know as well as I do that she's not going to make it."

Kat wanted to berate him. She wanted to say that he was tired, that he was depressed because of his long illness, that he wasn't being fair. But deep in her heart, she knew that she agreed with him. Rachel had said that she'd be home by noon, and it was already almost four. For the hundredth time, Kat wondered what her sister's friends had been counting down. How many more drinks had they downed to celebrate whatever it was? What else had they consumed, substances stronger than alcohol?

Before Kat could figure out an appropriate reply to her father, Susan left a cluster of her friends and came to join them on the bench. "Kat! Lauren says she saw your flyer in every store on Main Street. I can't tell you how many people told me how professional it looks."

Kat smiled automatically, but there was a chill beneath her reaction. Sure, the paperwork looked good. The class rosters were filling up. But she *still* hadn't broached the subject of the bank account with her mother. Every day that passed made Kat more worried, but no matter how many times she promised herself, she just couldn't find the words to deliver the bad news. She felt like she was living a lie, every time she talked about the studio but stayed silent about the money.

Before Kat could respond to Susan's compliment, Niffer came skidding to a stop in front of them. "The game's about to start! Is Mommy here yet?" The child craned her neck, peering around at the benches as if a full-grown woman might somehow be hiding nearby.

Susan answered for all of them. "Not yet, dear. Oh, look! Coach Noah is looking for you."

Niffer, though, directed her eyes over Kat's shoulder. "Mr. Harmon! Guess what! My mommy is coming to see me play today!"

Rye felt like someone had kicked him in his gut as he watched Niffer run back to the T-ball diamond. Rachel? Here?

His hands instinctively flexed into fists, as if he needed to defend himself in some battle. He wasn't ready to see Rachel. Not yet.

After walking out of the Chamber of Commerce dinner the night before, he had spent the entire night thinking about Josh's revelation. He'd tossed and turned on his mattress, tangling himself in his sheets until he swore and got up to splash cold water on his face.

How had he not seen the truth before? Why had he let Rachel's lies derail him? Why hadn't Rachel come after him for child support? And how was he going to tell Kat the truth? How could he tell Niffer?

Over and over, he asked himself what Rachel had possibly hoped to gain, keeping him in the dark.

But it all made sense, in a twisted way. Rachel thrived on drama. In her heart of hearts, she had to know that Rye would have stepped up, faced his responsibility. Rye would have done everything he could to help Rachel, to ease Niffer's strange, unbalanced life.

But Rachel could get far more mileage out of Josh being Niffer's father. She could sulk about being rejected by the guy who'd made it big. She could complain about the vast wealth that should have been hers. She could lash out against a system that had cheated her, denied her rights, cast her loose. And Josh wasn't around Eden Falls often enough to bother setting the record straight.

Rye had to figure out what was right, how he could take responsibility for Niffer now, at this relatively late date. But to do that, he needed to talk to Rachel. Rachel, who Niffer had just sunnily proclaimed was coming to the park.

Shoving down the feeling that his world was rapidly spinning out of control, Rye forced himself to smile at an unsuspecting Kat, to shake hands with Mike. Susan made a big show of coming over to kiss him on his cheek, to tell him how pleased she was about the renovations he'd completed at the dance studio. A quick glance from Kat reminded him of the cover story they'd concocted. According to the lies, Rye had just come in to freshen up the paint, to update the appearance of the Morehouse Dance Academy. Susan was never to know how badly Rachel had managed the business.

He forced himself to smile and make small talk with Kat's mother.

Rachel's mother, too.

What the hell was he going to do when she showed up? For all he knew, she might be in one of her crazy moods. If she saw that Kat and Rye were together, she might announce their past relationship to the entire world, trumpet it to the heavens for all to hear, just to see how everyone reacted.

He could only imagine the look that Kat would turn on him then. He could picture the hurt in her eyes, almost as clearly as if he already saw it. Sure, he had already told Kat that he'd dated her sister for a few weeks. But he'd purposely kept the extent of that "dating" vague. He certainly hadn't given a hint that a child could have resulted from that brief time together.

He needed a break to think this through. "Excuse me," he said. "I'm going to grab a hot dog before the game."

"I'll come with you," Kat chimed in, smiling. His heart sank, but he gave her a hand as she stepped down from the benches. He regretted how easily she twined her fingers between his, how comfortably she fell into step beside him as they made their way to the edge of the park.

Kat deserved better than this. She deserved more from him than being mortally embarrassed when her sister walked into the middle of this supposedly perfect spring afternoon.

"It's going to be okay," Kat said, as soon as they were out of earshot from her parents.

Rye started when she spoke, almost as if he were a child caught stealing cookies from the cooling rack. "What will?" he choked out.

"This whole thing with Rachel. We've tried to let Niffer know that she can't rely on her mother, that just because Rachel *said* she'd be here today, doesn't mean it's going to happen. It's so hard, though. Niffer hears what she wants to hear. I guess all kids do. The whole time we were walking over here, Niffer kept telling us that she's going to hit three home runs, just for Rachel. As if Noah could have coached her on how to do *that*." They walked another few steps in silence before she said, "That was sort of like a joke, Rye."

He shook his head, looking at her as if he were truly seeing her for the first time that day. "I'm sorry. I guess I'm a little preoccupied."

"We all have been. It's one thing for us adults to know we can't depend on Rachel. It's another for Niffer to learn the truth." She squeezed his hand gently. "I'm really touched that you're taking this so hard. It means a lot to me that you care so much about Niffer."

There, Rye thought. That was the opening he was looking for. That was the introduction he needed to tell Kat what was really on his mind.

But could he do that to her? Before he'd had a chance to talk to Rachel himself, to confirm the facts one last time? And could he break the news to Kat here, in full view of half the town, with an innocent T-ball game starting up behind them? He could already hear the children's shouts, the good-natured cheering for the kids at bat, for the ones in the field. And Kat was already wound so tight, worried about how Niffer would cope when Rachel didn't show.

When Rachel didn't show. Despite Niffer's heart-stopping announcement, Kat didn't think that Rachel was going to make it to the game. In fact, from the look on Mike's face, the man had been pretty certain his other daughter was a no-show. Come to think of it, even Susan had looked unsure.

Well, if Rachel didn't come to the park today, then Rye's secret was safe for a while longer. He could still track her down, get absolute confirmation. Then he could choose his time and his place. He could break things to Kat gently.

Hunching his shoulders, he folded his misery deeper into the nauseating sea of his emotions. He *would* clean this up. He had to. But this was neither the time, nor the place.

"Want a hot dog?" he asked, pulling out his wallet.

"You have got to be kidding." Kat laughed. "Do you know how bad those things are for you?"

"Worse than a burger and fries?" he retorted.

That did the trick. He knew that she was immediately thinking of the booth they had shared at the Garden Diner, of the meal that she had enjoyed with so much primal enthusiasm. Of the passion that had followed, on her couch. And, if her memory worked anything like his, of the follow-through in her bedroom, just a few days before.

"You should be careful," he said, lathering mock concern over his words. "It looks like you're getting a sunburn."

He supposed that he really did deserve the punch that she delivered to his shoulder. It was worth it, to get another look at the blush on her cheeks. He leaned closer, whispered in her ear, "Do you blush all over? Head to toe?"

He loved the little squealing noise she made in protest. He relished the thought that she would make him pay for his impertinence. Later. In private.

As much as Kat enjoyed sitting next to Rye on the bench, basking in the sun and watching the kids play ball, she felt her stomach twist into knots as the innings crept by. She caught herself glancing at her watch for the third time in as many minutes.

It was nearly five o'clock.

Kat caught Niffer looking worriedly at the stands as she came up to bat for the last time. Rye made a point of waving spiritedly to the little girl, starting up a chant. "Niff-er! Niff-er!" The child seemed to perk up at his attention, lifting her chin in a show of athletic determination. Kat almost laughed—her niece seemed to have learned the gesture from her sometime coach.

The bat cracked against the ball, and Niffer took off around the bases. When she stopped at second, she dusted off her hands, looking every bit a pro. Kat's heart almost broke, though, when the child shielded her eyes, gazing plaintively back at the stands.

Another three batters, and the game was over; Niffer's team had won by two runs. Each child trotted out toward the pitcher's mound, shaking hands with the opposition, as if they'd competed in the Olympics. Niffer joined in the group cheer that rounded out the game, and then she raced back to the benches.

"Where's Mommy?" she asked, craning her neck for a better view. "Did Mommy see me bat?"

Mike's face was creased with a mixture of anger and

fatigue. Susan sighed deeply. Kat held out her arms, ready to gather in her disappointed niece. But it was Rye who said, "Sorry, Niffer, your mother didn't come." His tone was matter-of-fact.

"But she said she would be here!"

"She must have made a mistake." Kat was grateful that Rye was being so reasonable, that he was speaking to Niffer as if she were an intelligent person, capable of handling an emotional blow. Anything else, and Kat was afraid that *she* would lose her own firm resolve to stay cheerful.

"Grown-ups don't make mistakes!" Niffer whined.

Grown-ups make mistakes all the time, Rye wanted to say. He felt as if his heart was breaking as he faced the result of his own biggest mistake.

Because Niffer's disappointment was yet another consequence of what he'd done with Rachel. If he had insisted on proof, way back when, if he had forced Rachel to share the results of the paternity test, then Niffer would not be so bereft today. She would have known all along that she had one loving parent to watch her accomplishments, to cheer her on.

Unable to say the words that would make everything right, he tried to do the next best thing. Pulling Niffer close to his side, he rubbed her narrow back with a sympathetic hand. "I'm sorry, kiddo. I wish your mommy had made it." He didn't. Not at all. Not yet. But he could fake the words well enough to fool a child. "I can think of one thing that might make everything better."

Niffer dug the toe of her sneaker into the ground, obviously reluctant to accept any comfort. "What?"

"How about an ice-cream cone?" That got her attention. "You can get yours with sprinkles."

"And a cherry on top?"

"Yeah. I think we can manage that." He looked up at the semicircle of adults. "Who's up for ice cream?"

Mike cleared his throat. "I think it's about time for me to head home. It's been a long day."

Susan chimed in immediately. "That makes two of us. That was such an exciting game, Niffer! Thank you for inviting us."

Mike took his time managing the two short steps from the bleachers to the ground. Rye offered him a steady forearm to balance against as he dropped the final few inches. The older man leaned close, clapping Rye on the back. "Thank you, son." The grim look in Mike's watery blue eyes let Rye know that the thanks were for more than a helping hand. "Thank you for taking care of my girls."

Kat's father wouldn't be so grateful if he knew the full story.

For that matter, neither would Kat. Rye's belly tightened as he caught her appreciative smile.

Kat waited until her parents were well on their way across the park before she turned back to her niece. "Okay, Niffer. Go get your glove, and thank Coach Noah." The little girl ran off. Kat looked at Rye. "You don't have to do this, you know."

"I want to."

"I've had a lifetime of being disappointed by my sister. Niffer had better get used to it. And I can assure you, you don't want to get wrapped up in this particular drama. It just repeats itself, over and over and over. Steer as far away as you can get."

"I'm already involved," Rye said, his voice deadly earnest.

Kat half expected him to make a joke as he said the

words. Well, not a joke exactly, but some friendly gesture of comfort, a sly side comment that would make her blush, something that would make her wish that there were a lot more days left in the spring, that New York and Richmond were not so very far apart.

But there was no secret message behind Rye's statement. There was no hidden tweak. He was stating a fact as bare as the red earth of the pitcher's mound behind him—he *was* already involved. He'd become involved the instant that she'd let him drive her home from the train station, the moment that he'd offered to renovate the studio. The second that she had leaned against him in the kitchen, pulling him close for that deeper kiss, for that soul-shocking meld that had echoed through the past couple of weeks, culminating in the afternoon they'd spent in bed—was it already four days before?

He looked like he was thinking of saying something else, but Niffer came bouncing back, glove in hand. "Can I get mint chocolate chip?"

Rye said, "If they have it."

"What flavor are you getting, Aunt Kat?"

Kat smiled and ruffled her niece's hair. "I don't eat ice cream, sweetheart."

"Never?" Niffer's eyes got very big.

"Never."

Niffer scrunched up her nose. "Do you eat ice cream, Mr. Harmon?"

"Every chance I get," he said, making the little girl laugh. "My favorite is coffee mint mango crunch."

"That's not a real flavor!"

"Hmm," Rye said, as if he were considering the matter for the very first time. "Maybe I'll just get butter pecan, then."

As they drew close to the truck, Niffer said, "Mr. Harmon, why don't you let Aunt Kat drive?"

Rye's laugh was short. "That's a great idea. What do you think, Aunt Kat? Want to get behind the wheel?"

Kat shot daggers at him with her eyes. "No, thank you," she said, making her voice as cold as the ice cream the others were about to enjoy. She couldn't resist adding a sarcastic edge. "But I really appreciate your asking."

"My pleasure," Rye said mildly.

He should know better than that, trying to egg her on in front of her niece. There was absolutely no way she was going to get behind the wheel of the silver truck. She was no idiot. She'd learned her lesson, in no uncertain terms. Only after she and Niffer were strapped into their seat belts did she think to ask, "Why do you care so much about whether I know how to drive, Niffer?"

"That's what grown-ups *do*," the child said, as if the concept were as simple as one plus one. "I'm just a kid, so I need to have a grown-up take care of me. Gram and Pop-pop and Mommy don't love me anymore, but I thought that *you* could be my grown-up. You know. Forever." Niffer had spoken matter-of-factly, but her lower lip started to tremble as she looked out the window. "But you can't do it, Aunt Kat, because you don't know how to drive."

"Oh, sweetheart!" Kat folded her niece into a hug, looking hopelessly at Rye as he pulled out of the parking lot. He seemed to be concerned about the traffic on the road; all of his attention was riveted on the cars that streamed by. She had no idea where to start unpacking all the misunderstandings in what the child had said. "Gram and Pop-pop love you very much, but they need their house to be quiet right now, so that Pop-pop can keep getting better. Your mommy loves you, too, but she just can't be with you now. And grown-ups can take care of you, even if they don't know how to drive. *I* can take care of you."

"Will you be my forever grown-up?"

Kat's throat swelled closed with the sudden threat of tears. "Forever is a very long time, Niffer. I can promise you this. You'll never be left alone. You'll have a grown-up to help you for as long as you need someone. Okay?"

Niffer's dark eyes were very serious, as if she were weighing every syllable of Kat's vow. "Okay," she said at last.

As soon as they arrived at the ice-cream parlor, Niffer saw a friend, and she ran across the room, squealing with delight, their serious conversation completely forgotten. "Yikes," Kat said to Rye as they took their place in line. "I had no idea how to respond to that!"

Yikes, indeed, Rye thought. It had been everything he could do not to stop the truck right there in the parking lot. Not to turn to Kat and Niffer and make his confession. Not to tell them the whole truth, get the horrible weight off his chest, shed it from around his heart.

Of course, he didn't say anything. Niffer would only be confused by what he had to say. The child was fragile enough, without witnessing her aunt's justified, unbridled rage. And Kat would—rightfully—be furious when she learned what had happened. And there was still a chance—a tiny one, but a chance nonetheless—that Rachel would tell him something different when he finally tracked her down, that she would have some other explanation, some proof.

But there was something else. Something he had only just started to work out for himself.

He didn't want to lose Kat, didn't want to miss out on her gorgeous smile, her easy companionship, the unrivaled excitement that she brought to their shared bed. Sure, they seemed great together. But she *was* heading back to New York soon, with or without Rye's big confession. He was going to lose her to the big city, to her life with the ballet—there had never been any other possible ending for their story together. This reckless spring was going to be a memory, probably in a week, maybe less.

Was it really so terrible to let Kat go without knowing the truth about him and Rachel? Was it the end of the world if she went back to her real life thinking fondly of Rye, of the time they had shared in Eden Falls?

Everything would be different, of course, if he had any chance of keeping her with him. But Kat was never going to come live with him in Richmond. She'd never trim her wings and settle for a second-rate city. Not when she could have it all in New York. And he had absolutely no basis for building a business in Manhattan.

It was only fair to Kat that he keep quiet—just for another week or two. Once she was safely in her real life, Rye would face the music. He'd step up and accept his responsibility, treat Niffer like his daughter, make sure that she was safe forever, that all her needs were met. There was just no need to make a formal acknowledgment now. No reason to ruin the short time that Kat had left in Eden Falls. This was a kindness to her. Really.

Rye resolved to ignore the headache that started

pounding behind his eyes as he ran through his justifi-
cations one more time.

Niffer came skipping to the counter when they
neared the front of the line. Kat was pleased to see that
Rye had finally relaxed after the tension of Rachel's
no-show. He laughed as he ordered up Niffer's mint
chocolate chip, complete with the mandatory sprinkles
and cherry. Rye's own butter-pecan cone followed. He
passed the ice cream to her so that he could pull his
wallet out of his pocket.

Maybe it was the fragrance of the butter-rich ice
cream. Maybe it was the freshly made waffle cone.
Maybe it was the bright sunshine outside, or the emotional dam she had just built for Niffer. But suddenly
Kat found herself saying to the woman behind the
counter, "And I'll have a scoop of chocolate, please."

"Cone or cup?"

Cup was safest. No more calories. No greater threat
to her dancer fitness.

But this was the first time she'd had ice cream in
years. "Waffle cone, please." Rye laughed and paid the
total.

"Aunt Kat!" Niffer said as they sat down at a tiny
metal table. "You got ice cream!"

"I couldn't let you have all the fun, could I?" She
licked her cone, and the ice cream melted across her
tongue, cold and rich and satisfying. She laughed in
pure enjoyment, marveling at the simple pleasure she
had denied herself for so long. Niffer joined in, and Rye
wasn't far behind. Before long, Kat couldn't even have
said what was so funny. What was so perfect. All she
knew was that *this* was living, *this* was embracing the
world in a way that she had almost forgotten how to do.

They finished their treats and walked back to the

truck. Before Rye could open the door, a siren began to wail in the distance. Kat automatically looked around for the source, and she spotted a huge fire engine, barreling down the road. The deep horn boomed as the truck approached the intersection, making Niffer huddle against her hip. "It's okay," Kat said automatically. Nevertheless, she held her niece close until the truck had disappeared.

"Hmm," Kat mused, as Rye turned the key in the ignition. "That's the first siren I've heard since I came to Eden Falls. Back in New York, I hear a dozen before breakfast."

"A dozen fire trucks?" Niffer asked.

"Some fire trucks. And police cars and ambulances, too. You can hear the noise all day long. All night, too." Even as Kat thought about it, she realized that her nights had been peaceful in Eden Falls. In fact, she routinely fell asleep as soon as her head hit the pillow, and she slept so soundly that she couldn't remember her dreams in the morning.

Not like New York, at all. Back in the noisy apartment that she shared with Haley, she woke up nearly once an hour. If it wasn't sirens, it was barking dogs, or screeching garbage trucks, or noisy people on the street, six floors below. Even when Kat *did* sleep in New York, she was disturbed by vivid dreams, by nightmares that jolted her awake as she imagined tumbling off a stage, or breaking her leg when her partner failed to catch her after some dramatic leap.

Maybe that was why her foot had healed so fast here in Eden Falls. She was sleeping well for the first time in years.

Speaking of which… "Okay, Niffer. As soon as we

get home, I want you changing into your nightgown and brushing your teeth. Got it?"

"Got it!" The little girl was already yawning as Rye pulled into the driveway.

Kat took extra care tucking Niffer into bed. She smoothed the sheets carefully, folding them so that they weren't too high on the child's chest. She kissed Niffer on her forehead, switched on the night-light, told her to "Sleep tight!" She sat beside Niffer's bed, watching as the little girl's frown smoothed out, as her breathing evened, as she slipped deep into sleep.

Will you be my forever grown-up? Kat's heart seized at the earnestness behind Niffer's question.

Rye was waiting in the living room.

"I am going to murder my sister," she said, whispering so that Niffer couldn't hear.

For answer, Rye held out his arms. She let him fold her close to his chest. His shirt smelled of sunlight and spring air and something that was indefinably, unmistakably *Rye*. His arms tightened around her, carving out a refuge, making her feel safe. She felt his lips brush against the crown of her head.

"I'm sorry," he murmured.

She wanted to tell him that it wasn't his fault. She wanted to tell him that Rachel had always been a flake, that Kat truly could not remember a time when she had been able to trust her sister to keep a promise. She wanted to tell him that she was grateful for all that he had done, for coming to the game, for treating them to ice cream. For coming inside now, and for holding her close.

She pulled back enough that she could look up at his face, and all the need for words disappeared. Instead, he touched his lips to hers, sudden urgency overtaking his initial chaste sweetness. Kat laced her fingers between his and led him toward her bed.

Chapter Eight

Kat flexed her left ankle and walked across the dance studio floor. "I can't believe it," she said to her mother. "My foot feels so light!" She glared at the bright blue boot she had just removed.

"Are you sure you should be walking on it?" Susan fussed.

"The X-rays came back fine. Daddy's surgeon said that he could barely see where the original fracture was." That morning, Kat had insisted on visiting her father's doctor. Her foot felt entirely healed; she could not remember the last time she'd felt a twinge of pain. It was time to be shed of the boot.

Still, Susan shook her head. "I worry about you, Kat."

"Mama, I'm fine."

"You push yourself too hard. You always have. At least you've taken a bit of time off while you've been here. It seems like you and that Harmon boy are getting along quite well."

Kat laughed at her mother's not-so-subtle hint, even as she felt her cheeks flush crimson. "No, Mama," she said, meeting Susan's eyes in the mirror. "I *don't* have anything to tell you about Rye and me."

"I wasn't asking!"

"Of course not."

"It's just that I like seeing you happy. I understand that you actually had an ice-cream cone, when he took you and Niffer out after the game?"

"Who told you that?"

"Teresa Rodriguez saw the three of you sitting at a table."

"Does every single detail of everybody's life get broadcast in this town?" Kat tried to sound annoyed, but she was actually quite amused. Susan looked as pleased as a well-fed cat that she had gleaned information about Kat's not-date.

"Not every detail, dear. Teresa couldn't remember if you ordered chocolate or coffee crunch."

Kat's mock frown twisted into a laugh. "You know me. Chocolate was always my favorite. It's Rachel who likes coffee crunch."

"That's right," Susan agreed. "Besides, Teresa wasn't really reporting on ice-cream flavors. She was much more interested in telling me about your boyfriend."

"Rye isn't my boyfriend," Kat said, but she spat out the words a trifle too quickly. She wouldn't have believed herself, if she'd been on the receiving end of that denial. She tried to change the topic. "He *has* done a great job here, hasn't he?"

Susan looked around her studio, her fond smile testifying that she knew exactly what her daughter was doing. "I don't remember the last time the place looked so fine. We should be able to earn back all the lost income by autumn."

Kat's heart stuttered over a few beats. "Lost income?" she asked, as if she'd never heard the words before.

"Those checks from the fall session that Rachel never deposited? The money from spring and all those classes she let fall by the wayside?"

Susan sounded perfectly complacent as she enumerated her other daughter's shortcomings. Kat had rehearsed those words, over and over in her own mind. She'd tried to figure out how to say them simply, without affect, without any hint of the outrage that churned inside her whenever she thought of Rachel's failings. All that time Kat had rehearsed, but Susan had already known the lines. "Mama! When did you find out?"

Susan shrugged. "I've known all along. I kept hoping Rachel would pull herself together, that she'd get the money deposited for autumn term. Every day, I meant to ask her about the checks, to tell her that she wasn't being fair, failing to get the money to the bank. I never got around to it, though, with everything getting so crazy after your father got sick."

"She had an obligation to you, Mama! To the studio!"

Susan's smile reflected a lifetime of quiet hope, decades of constantly readjusting her expectations. "I knew what was going on. Fairness to me wasn't an issue. I never should have counted on Rachel to pull together an entire set of classes for spring. She's never had any interest in dance."

"She didn't have to be interested in dance! She had to be interested in *you!* In you and Daddy! She had to be interested in our family and do whatever she could to help out."

Susan shook her head sadly. "We both know that's not Rachel's strong suit, is it?"

"I don't think Rachel *has* a strong suit," Kat countered. Even as she said the spiteful words, though, she held up a hand. She didn't want to fight with her mother, to force a conversation about difficult things. "Forget I said that," she apologized. "But I still can't believe she just did nothing. That she let the studio fall apart like that."

"It wasn't all her fault, dear. I looked the other way. I knew the classes weren't going forward, and I let that happen. Sure, there were some disappointed little dancers...I know that. But I spoke to as many of the parents as I could, explained what was going on. Most of them already knew, of course. They were stopping by to bring meals, keeping me company at the hospital."

"But it didn't have to come to this! You should have called me back in December, when you first realized that things weren't on track for the spring term. I could have straightened things out before they ever got this bad!"

"And missed *Nutcracker?*"

The question cut like a knife. Of course Kat wouldn't have wanted to miss *The Nutcracker Suite.* She had been featured as the Sugar Plum Fairy. But now that she realized Susan had known what was happening, that Susan had been fully aware of how her lifetime's investment in the studio was fading away to nothing under Rachel's lazy management... "Mama, I would have come here in an instant. You know that."

"I know, dear. And honestly, that's why I didn't call

you. It's not fair that you should always be dragged in to clean up the messes that your sister leaves behind."

Susan sounded so sad, so utterly bereft, that Kat didn't know how to respond. She tried: "Mama, I've been so worried. I couldn't figure out how to tell you that the account was going to be low. I kept picturing you writing out a check and only then finding out that you had nothing left in the bank. The more I imagined it, the worse it became!"

"I keep a better eye on my checkbook than that, dear!"

"I know—or, at least, I always thought you did. I just figured that with Daddy so sick, and you so distracted, you hadn't even realized what was happening. I think I started to write you a hundred different letters, outlining everything and offering to help in any way that I could."

Susan shook her head. "I'm sorry this was all so stressful for you, dear. You should know by now—honesty is the best policy."

"Well I *do* know that, in general. But because Rachel was involved, I just felt like…" She trailed off, unsure of how she wanted to finish that statement.

"You just felt like you had to protect your sister."

Hearing those words brought tears to Kat's eyes. She *did* feel like she had to protect Rachel. Or, rather, she *had* felt that way. Now she was tired of covering for her twin, tired of spinning out reassurances and lies. It had taken twenty-four years, but Kat was finally ready to accept that she and Rachel were completely separate people. She wasn't responsible for the bad decisions that Rachel made. She couldn't change them, couldn't make them right.

"I'm sorry, Mama," she said, and it was an apology for all the things she'd said, and all the things she hadn't.

"Your father and I will always love both you girls. But we aren't blind. We see what Rachel has done with her life. It's taken us both a number of years, but we accept that we can't do anything to change that. To change her. The most we can do is to make sure that her daughter is taken care of, that an innocent child has the comfort and stability to grow into the person she is meant to be."

Kat thought of Niffer's matter-of-fact statement on the way to get ice cream, the child's certainty that she wasn't loved. "Niffer's a good girl, but she doesn't understand what's going on here. She's afraid she's going to be abandoned."

A shadow ghosted over Susan's face. "Your father and I worried about that when we asked you to come down here. We knew that Niffer would think we were pushing her away. But we hoped that she would find new strength with you, that she would realize there was yet another person who loves her, who wants to see her succeed. And in our wildest dreams, we never imagined that your father would recover so quickly, once the house settled down a little."

"I think I was too tough on Niffer when I first got here. I made her follow too many rules."

"Nonsense," Susan said. "The proof is in the pudding. That child is better than she's been in months."

Kat nodded. She'd seen Niffer's improvement. She'd seen the difference that her presence had made. And that was why Kat had reached a decision.

When she'd arrived in Eden Falls, Kat had planned on staying seven days, maybe ten. Those days, though, had stretched into weeks. And somewhere along the way, Kat had told herself a secret—she had decided to stay for even longer. She was going to stay in Eden Falls forever.

What had she told her mother, way back when she first came to town? She would leave the National Ballet Company the instant that dancing stopped being fun.

Sure, she had planned on dancing in New York for the rest of her life. She *knew* the company, understood the way it worked, knew its system in her very bones. She had set her goals, developed her strategies, lived by her very detailed rules. But somewhere along the way, it had stopped being fun. It had taken its toll on her sleep, on her physical health, on her mental stability.

When was the last time she'd even thought of the company? When had she spoken with Haley? It had been at least a week. No, almost two. Somehow, ballet gossip had become less compelling while she worked on finalizing things here at the studio. The hundred and one backstage dramas that she and Haley usually shared had lost a little—no, a *lot*—of their appeal. Life had come to seem so much richer, here in Eden Falls.

Besides, Kat could never get in shape in time for the *Coppelia* auditions. Of course she had always wanted to dance Swanilda. She was perfect for the role. But she could not deny that she had lost some muscle mass, with her foot confined to a cast. And she'd put on a couple of pounds, indulging in real meals, like a real woman, spending time with a real family.

Before, that weight would have sent her to the workout room, driven her to exercise as if she were harried by a thousand demons. But not anymore. Not now that Kat had made up her mind.

Not now that she was going to be Niffer's forever grown-up.

Amanda and Susan would just have to get used to driving her around town. They wouldn't mind, really. Shared drives would be a chance for all of them to spend time together.

Once Kat made up her mind, she felt as light as air, as certain as she'd been of anything since she'd been fourteen years old, since she'd headed up to New York to seek her fortune. She turned to face her mother. "Mama, I have something to tell you. I think I've known it for a while. Since I realized that we needed someone to teach the Advanced Showcase for the spring term."

"Darling, I can—"

"No, Mama. You can't. But I can. And I want to. I want to stay in Eden Falls." She saw that Susan didn't believe her, didn't truly understand, but she laughed all the same. "This feels right to me, Mama."

"But New York… Everything you've worked for. Everything you've spent your entire life—"

"Not my entire life, Mama. I spent more years here, with you and Daddy, than I've spent in New York. And it's time for me to come home now." Kat surprised herself, realizing how wonderful those words sounded. "It's time. Come on, Mama. Let me show you the calendar I set up on your computer."

She couldn't say whether she laughed because of Susan's expression of pleased surprise, or because her body felt so light and balanced as she crossed the studio floor without the hated walking cast.

By Sunday, Kat's foot felt as strong as it had before her fracture. She had tried hard to limit her time at the barre, conscientiously keeping from stretching her practices into hours-long torture sessions. Nevertheless, she was overjoyed to find that her strength had rebounded so quickly.

The absence of the boot made it easier to carry food to the sprawling picnic tables in the park. It was Sunday—May Day and Eden Falls's traditional Family Day celebration. In honor of the spring festivities, Kat had worn a green blouse. She'd actually bought it for the occasion, dragooning Amanda into driving her to one of the tiny shops on Main Street. Her cousin had been only too happy to help her pick out something more appropriate than New York black. Eventually, she'd have to choose a whole new wardrobe.

For now, though, Kat wasn't worried about clothes. Instead, she was worried about balancing the pair of desserts she had made with Susan. The lemon chess pie was a family favorite, and Niffer had begged for blackberry cobbler. Kat suspected that the child really just wanted to eat spoonfuls of the traditional whipped-cream topping.

"Go ahead, Niffer," Kat said, as they arrived at the park. "Go play with the other kids."

"I don't know anyone."

"Of course you do. I can see three different kids on your T-ball team."

"Will you come with me?"

Kat started to sigh in exasperation, but she thought better of herself. If Niffer wanted an adult's company, that was a small enough gift that Kat could provide. "You go over there, and I'll come see you in a moment. I just need to set these things down."

Kat added the desserts to a picnic table that looked like it might break under the combined weight of all the baked goods. The city of Eden Falls certainly knew how to throw a party. Kat could already smell hot dogs and hamburgers cooking on five or six grills. Another table was laden with salads, and there had to be a half-dozen coolers scattered under the trees, full of soft drinks and sweet tea.

After snagging a diet soda for herself and making sure that Susan and Mike were similarly cared for, Kat went to uphold her promise to her niece. Niffer came running up as Kat approached the gravel-covered playground.

"We're bored!" the child announced.

"How can you be bored?" Kat shaded her eyes, gesturing at all of the playground equipment. "You have a castle, and swings and a slide!"

"We *always* play on those. We need a new game."

A new game. Niffer had no idea just how foolish she was, coming to *Kat* for a new game. Ballet was the only game Kat had known for years. Somehow, she didn't think the kids would be excited about completing a hundred pliés. Then again, they might really get into the grand battements—those were basically an invitation to kick anyone who got within striking distance.

Somewhere between thinking about leg warm-ups and arm stretches, though, Kat remembered something Susan had said, weeks before. She smiled mischievously at Niffer and said, "How about Magic Zoo?"

"What's that?" Niffer sounded suspicious. Nevertheless, a half-dozen kids drew closer. Kat was going to have to make this good.

"First of all, everyone has to choose an animal, something you can find at the zoo. Think of it, but don't tell anyone yet!" She waited while the children selected their guises for the game. Several closed their eyes, as if they were imagining an entire menagerie. What had Susan said? That Kat had played the game by selecting crayons out of a bucket? The colors were supposed to mean something…. Well, there weren't any crayons around, so Kat was just going to have to improvise.

"Okay. Everyone choose a number between one and five. Got it?" Every child nodded, as serious as if they were completing a military exercise. "Now, listen carefully. Each number is a different magical ability. I'm going to tell you the magical abilities, and then you'll have to figure out how your animal uses its special skill. Everyone is going to close their eyes while you do that, and I'm going to hide this…" Kat hadn't thought that far ahead. What was she going to hide? What could the kids hunt for in their imaginary game?

"This bandanna." Rye made the announcement from directly behind her. She spun around to face him, astonished that she hadn't heard him approach. He'd been up in Richmond for the past week, tied up in business meetings, cementing the details on half a dozen new projects that had grown out of his attending that Chamber of Commerce dinner.

She had phoned him a week ago, after talking to her mother.

She had told him about her decision, about her choice to stay in Eden Falls.

He'd been shocked into silence at first, and then he'd started to apologize, started to explain that he had to stay in Richmond, that his business was there. She had laughed and told him that she knew. She understood. It was horrible, rotten luck that she hadn't returned home before he had left, but there were only a couple of hours of freeway between them. Somehow, some way, they would make it work.

She'd even said: "Rye, I know how it's been before. I know there were women who tied you to Eden Falls. Who made you feel like you had to stay here. I'm not those women. It's never going to be that way between us."

His voice had thickened then, as if he were overwhelmed with some emotion. He'd cleared his throat, said her name, almost as if he were bracing himself to make some grand confession. But that was silly. There wasn't anything for him to confess.

She'd missed him fiercely for the past week—more than she could have imagined, just a month before. But now he was back in Eden Falls, for Family Day. He was standing beside her, lowering his voice as if he were telling the children ghost stories at a campfire. He brandished his crimson bandanna before the children's fascinated faces. "This bandanna can work magic spells," he said. "It belongs to a princess who is being held captive in a tower, locked in by an evil magician. The princess can only be rescued by someone smart enough and brave enough to find the bandanna and wear it."

Kat watched the children's eyes grow wide at the fairy tale that Rye spun. "Okay," she said. "Remember your numbers now. One means you can fly. Two lets you be invisible. Three lets you walk through walls. Four gives you the ability to change into another animal. And five…" She trailed off. What was a fifth magical ability? What else could she factor into the kids' game?

Rye picked up the instructions, as if he'd known them all along. "And five lets you read minds."

Perfect. Kat flashed him a smile before she said, "Okay. Everyone cover your eyes, while the evil magician hides the bandanna!" The kids took the responsibility seriously—they buried their faces in the crooks of their arms. Kat waited until Rye had crossed the playground, planted the bandanna in the shadows at the base of the slide and sidled back to her. "All right, animals!" she shouted. "I'm going to count to five. And when I finish, you'll all be in the Magic Zoo!"

She drew out the count dramatically, stretching out the numbers until she shouted, "Five!" The kids flew off, lumbering like invisible elephants, roaring like flying lions.

Rye laughed as they tumbled across the playground. "That should keep them busy for a while."

"That was the idea," Kat said smugly.

Rye was suddenly nervous, standing alone with Kat. Every night for the past week, he'd tried to reach Rachel, calling her cell phone, sending text messages. While waiting for a response, he'd worked on how to tell Kat the truth about Niffer. He'd started to phone Kat a dozen times, mapping out the words in his mind, figuring out every single thing he had to say, so that it would be proper, so that she would understand.

And every time, he found he just couldn't tell her over the phone. And now, in the park, surrounded by the Eden Falls Family Day celebration, he had to wait yet again.

The breeze carried a whiff of her honey-apricot scent toward him, and he couldn't help but take a step closer. "So," he said, after swallowing hard. "You're wearing green to celebrate your jailbreak?"

"Jailbreak?" She looked confused.

He nodded toward her foot. "The boot?"

"Finally!" She spun in a circle, laughing. "I can move again. I didn't realize how confining that thing was until I had it off. But I'm wearing green for my new life, here in Eden Falls. For spring."

"It looks great on you," he said. "It sets off the color of your eyes." He couldn't resist trailing his hand along the garment's sleeve, touching the fold on the inside of her elbow. The fabric was nearly as soft as the tender flesh it covered. He felt the shiver that rocketed through Kat's body, and he almost laughed out loud.

Before he could lower his voice, though, before he could think of something that would make her move one step closer, a tumble of kids frothed around them, like puppies overturning a basket.

"That was too easy!"

"We found the bandanna!"

"Hide it again!"

Rye laughed and nodded toward Niffer, who brandished the bandanna as if it were a carnival prize. "You go ahead and hide it now. Find a better place. You can use the whole park."

The kids shrieked with excitement, barely managing to cover their eyes. Niffer flew off toward the castle, intent on securing her treasure. Soon enough, the entire herd had thundered away again.

"So," Rye said, stepping closer to Kat. "Where were we?"

"I think I was about to tell you my foot is as good as new." She flexed one of her long legs, extending her toes in a graceful arch that defied the strappy sandals she wore.

Laughing, he closed his hands around her waist. "Wasn't this where we started, ten years ago? With you stretching that leg?" He pulled her close and slanted his lips over hers. He might need to keep this kiss clean enough for a public park, but there was no reason it had to be the fraternal gesture he had tried—and failed—to deliver years before.

"I guess it was," Kat whispered against his throat. "Even though I didn't realize we were starting *anything* that day." She settled her arms around his neck, relishing the feeling that he was claiming her, announcing that she was his, at least for today, for as long as they were both in Eden Falls. She caught her breath against a sudden pang at the thought of being separated from Rye, of losing him forever.

No. She had already told him this. It was best that he continue with his business in Richmond. He had planned so long, worked so hard. He would hate her forever, if she asked him to give up his dreams. That was why she'd been patient for the past week. Why she'd managed not to phone him every single night. She had to be content with everything she had—and do her best to lure him to Eden Falls, early and often. "I have an idea," she whispered against the corner of his mouth. "For how we might *end* this. At least for today."

He chuckled and pulled her closer.

Even as she started to remind him—remind them both—that they were standing in a public park, in broad daylight, there was the sound of one person clapping. The noise was sharp, irregular, and Kat whirled around, barely noticing that Rye's hand on her waist helped her keep her balance on the soft grass.

"What would Mom think, Kat? Should I go get her, so she can see what you're really like?"

Kat recognized the voice, even before her mind processed the old words. "Rachel," Kat said, the two syllables clattering between them like hail.

"Kat," her sister replied evenly. "Rye."

Kat stared into eyes that matched her own silver-gray. But those other eyes were rimmed with heavy eyeliner and multiple coats of mascara. And framed by hair that had been dyed a brilliant, unnatural magenta. Rachel had put on weight since the last time Kat had seen her; the line of her jaw was soft, and there were bags beneath her eyes. But there was no mistaking her twin. And no mistaking the oath that Rye muttered, barely under his breath.

"What are you doing here?" Kat asked, scarcely aware that her fingers were curling into fists.

"You were in the room when I called Mom and Dad. I said I'd visit my baby."

"You were supposed to be here a week ago. Niffer expected you at her T-ball game."

"Niffer?" Rachel's laugh was as harsh as fingernails on a chalkboard. "Who came up with that idiotic name?"

"I did." Rye stepped forward.

Rachel's eyes narrowed. "There was nothing wrong with Jenny."

Rye answered evenly, as if he were measuring out each word with the level in his tool kit. "Except for the fact that she hated it."

Rachel's old look of cunning crept across her face. A block of ice settled in Kat's belly, and she realized that there was another conversation going on in front of her, a whole set of words that she could not understand, dared not predict. "Rye?" she asked, her fingers clutching at his forearm. "What's going on here?"

"Yes," Rachel said. "Why don't you tell her what's going on, Rye?"

There it was again, that complicated flash of meaning between Kat's boyfriend and her twin. Rye's face was ironed into lean planes; she heard him swallow hard. When he spoke, the words were taut, pulled thin as wire. "I don't want to do this here, Rachel. Let's get out of the park, at least. We can talk at your parents' house."

"But Rye! It's Family Day!" Rachel's response was cold, mocking.

Of course Rachel was doing this. Rachel had caught Kat kissing Rye. She was jealous of something she could never, ever have. Rachel had always been that way, whenever she saw Kat succeeding. Kat started to make excuses to Rye, started to explain away her sister's bad behavior. The jagged look in Rye's eyes, though, froze her to the spot. There was more to Rachel's riposte than the sibling rivalry Kat had lived with all her life.

Before Kat could tease out the meaning of what was going on in front of her, a brightly colored bullet shot across the clearing. "Mommy!" Niffer screamed. "Mommy, you're here!"

"Of course, baby. How could your mother be anywhere else?" Rachel put a curious emphasis on the word *mother,* as if she were staking claim to the title for the very first time. Nevertheless, Kat watched Rachel pull away from her daughter's clutching fingers, saw Rachel glare at Rye as if *he* were responsible for Niffer's clinginess.

Rachel's gaze was momentarily obscured by a cloud of Niffer's jet-black hair. Jet-black hair, like Kat's own. Like Rachel's, when it wasn't dyed.

But Niffer had eyes to match that hair. Eyes far darker than Kat's, than Rachel's. Eyes as dark as Rye's.

And as Kat looked more closely, she saw other resemblances, as well. The line of Niffer's jaw. The tilt of her nose. The way that she clutched a red bandanna, tight in her left hand.

Left.

Like Rye.

Suddenly, everything was bright around the four of them, as if they were illuminated from within. There was a buzz in Kat's ears, a humming sound. The roof of her mouth had gone numb, and she realized that her fingertips were tingling. She felt isolated from the world. Cut off. Alone.

"You're her father," Kat said.

Those three words jolted through Rye like a bolt cutter.

His first response was relief. At last, his secret was out. He was through with the lies, done with the stupid disclosure he'd been struggling to make since Josh had told him the truth.

His second response, though, was sickening fear. The color had drained from Kat's cheeks; she looked like she had seen a ghost.

He should have found a way to tell Kat sooner. He should have owned the situation instead of waiting for her to uncover it this way. If he'd stepped up to the plate, he could have broken the news more gently, explained everything more completely. Even over the phone—he could have protected her, guided her, made her see how this had happened.

Well, he hadn't chosen the time or the place, but he could still make Kat understand. Tenderly, he reached out to take her arm, to guide her toward the nearest bench.

She pulled away from him as if his hands were acid. "Don't touch me!" she snapped. Her voice was high.

Broken. She sounded as if she were fracturing into a million jagged pieces.

"Kat, it was a long time ago." He pitched his voice low, unconsciously slipping into the comforting register that he would use for an injured animal, for a sick child.

"Rachel is my *sister*." Kat's eyes were wide, unfocused. "You slept with my *sister!*"

Of course, what she said was true, the bare words. But there were a dozen things wrong with that sentence, a hundred ways that the facts failed to capture the reality. Starting with: "It was six years ago. We only dated for a few weeks."

"You told me that! But you never said you *slept* with her!"

Rye glared at Rachel, at the pink-haired harpy that was laughing at him over the head of her distraught daughter. "Tell her, Rachel. Tell her that it never meant anything."

Impossibly, Rachel was throwing back her head to laugh. But no. That wasn't *impossible*. Rachel had been manipulating Kat for years. Manipulating him, as well, even when he hadn't realized they were enmeshed in a game.

Now Rachel settled a hand over her daughter's— *their* daughter's—head. "I don't know, Rye," she said. "I wouldn't say that it never meant *anything*."

A strangled sound caught at the back of Kat's throat. Instinctively, Rye glanced around to see who was watching them. The kids were all playing at the far end of the park, shouting and running around in circles. A couple of the adults had glanced their way, but no one was close enough to hear. Kat whispered, "Were you planning on telling me anytime soon, Rye?"

"I didn't know… I only found out last week."

Rachel laughed—a harsh bark. "Not very observant, then, were you?"

"You stay out of this!" He would have said more, would have lashed out with the anger that flashed through his chest, but he saw Niffer cringe against her mother's side. He forced himself to lower his voice, and he bit out the words, "Rachel, you are not helping here."

"It's not my job to help you, is it?"

"Mommy?" Niffer whispered, but her question was perfectly clear. "Why is Mr. Harmon angry?"

"I don't know, baby," Rachel said, her voice as sweet as molasses dregs. "I think because he was caught lying to Aunt Kat."

"Gram says it's bad to tell a lie."

Rachel's laugh was loud, like the call of a raucous jay. "Yes, baby. Telling a lie is definitely bad."

Rye thought his heart would break as Niffer turned toward him, her jet-black eyes enormous in her pale face. "You shouldn't tell lies, Mr. Harmon."

"It wasn't a lie," he said, before he'd thought out a way to explain all of this to a child. "It was more of a… secret." As Rachel laughed again, Rye turned to Kat. The color had come back to her face with a vengeance; her cheeks were spotted with two hectic patches. He could hear her breath coming in short pants, and she hugged herself like a wounded creature. "Kat," he said. "Let me explain."

Kat heard his plea, and her belly twisted into a pulsing knot. Even so, she felt disconnected from her body, cut loose from the arms and legs and heart that she was so used to working, every minute of every day. Her hurt and fury cut her off from herself, like a shimmering electric curtain. She wasn't certain where her words came from, where she found the strength to ask, "What could you possibly have to say? How could you possibly have forgotten to mention something so important?"

It wasn't fair. It had never been fair. Rachel had always gotten her own way, done whatever she wanted to do, and damn the consequences. Rachel had never bothered with goals, with strategies. Rachel had always broken the rules. Rachel had lied to Susan and Mike all her life, lied to Kat, lied to her own daughter, Niffer.

Why *Rye?* Of all the men that Rachel could have had, why did it have to be Rye?

Kat's thoughts collapsed in on themselves, sending up embers of memories. She was back in the high school auditorium, her cheeks wet with tears of adolescent frustration, with shame at being laughed at by the high school kids. She was staring at Rye, confused by his kiss, even as she was delighted by the tenderness he had shown her.

She'd been mortified to find her sister waiting for her, embarrassed to hear that Susan was waiting outside, ready to drive them both home. Rachel had eyed Kat with a knowing expression. Rachel had bided her time, never telling Susan and Mike what she'd seen backstage in the high school auditorium. Rachel had known even then, even when they were in eighth grade, that she was going to set her hat for Rye Harmon.

But Rachel couldn't have done it alone. She couldn't have broken Kat's heart without an accomplice. She couldn't have turned Kat's life upside down without Rye playing along.

"Rye," Kat said, and her heart was breaking. "How could you?"

He sighed, unsure of the answer, even as he knew he

had to find one. "I swear I didn't know, Kat. Not until last week."

"Last *week?* You admitted that you dated her, but it went a bit beyond that, didn't it? A *lot* beyond that."

"I should have told you everything. I didn't think it mattered." He hadn't wanted it to matter.

Kat shook her head vehemently, clearly rejecting his excuses. "Where?" she demanded. "Where did you sleep with her?"

There wasn't any good answer, nothing that would help Kat to understand. "It doesn't matter."

"Was it in her house? Rye, were you on her couch? In her bedroom?" Kat twisted her mouth around the ugly questions.

Rye knew that she had to be picturing the room where they had embraced, where he had first realized the fragility of the soul inside her steel. Even now, he could picture Kat's mouth open in a perfect O of ecstasy as she shuddered beneath him, as she rode the waves of pleasure that he had given to her—*her*—because she was the woman he wanted to be with. She was the woman he loved.

The woman he loved. The realization tore through him, dragging him away from the perfection of memories, pushing him back to the terrible, horrible *now*. He loved Kat, and he had somehow managed to hurt her more than he had ever hurt anyone before. He shrugged helplessly, unable to imagine words that would reassure her.

Tears streamed down her cheeks, and her breath came in short gasps. "I thought we were working together, Rye."

"We were!"

Rachel chortled at his protest, even as Niffer asked her mother what was going on.

Kat could not believe Rye. Not when his secrets involved Rachel. Not when they involved the sister who had let her down—let her entire family down—so many times in the past. Kat laughed herself, but there was no humor behind her words. "I fell for everything, didn't I? Hook, line and sinker. Oh my God, I am so stupid!"

"Kat, you know that isn't true. Listen to me. This doesn't have to change anything between us. This doesn't have to be the end."

"Really? Rye Harmon, why should I believe anything you say, ever again?" Her words chased after each other, tumbling from her lips as if they had a life of their own. She was hurt. She was embarrassed. She was utterly terrified that Rye was telling her the truth now, and she feared that he was not. She didn't know what to believe, not anymore. Not after she'd been so blind.

The only way she could protect herself, the only way she could defend the wounded perimeter of her heart, was to lash out—fast, and furious, and with the sharpest weapon she had in her arsenal. "You don't know how to have a real relationship, do you, Rye? That's why you moved to Richmond in the first place. So that you wouldn't have to deal with *feelings,* with responsibility. Everything was fine between us, as long as we were both just having fun. But when things got serious, you shut down. When you learned the truth about Niffer, you stayed away—avoided me for an entire week! You chose Rachel and Richmond over Niffer, Rye. Over me."

How could she have let this happen?

Her mother had told her to be happy. Her mother had

told her to relax her rigid rules. Her mother had told her to take each day as it came, to enjoy herself.

And this was the result.

Kat had set her rules, years ago, for one simple reason. Rules protected her. Rules kept her safe. Rules preserved her from the jagged pain that was shattering her even now. She never should have relaxed her standards, never should have given in. She never should have let Rye take the fortress of her heart, of her solitude, of all the protective isolation she had built when she was a teenager.

"Kat, I never chose Rachel over you. I stayed in Richmond because I've spent the past week trying to figure out how to tell you the truth. You have to understand. I never meant to hurt you."

"But you did," she sobbed. "You really did, Rye. I thought we had something special. I thought there was a real connection between us. I thought you understood who I am, and what I want, what I *need*."

He had one last chance here. One final opportunity to use words to make it right. "I do, Kat. I promise you, I do."

She shook her head hard enough that her easy chignon fell loose about her face. "No! If you truly understood me, you would know that this is one thing that I can never, ever forgive."

He reached out for her, desperate to change her mind.

"Don't touch me!" That shout was loud enough to get attention. Out of the corner of his eye, Rye could see faces turn. He could measure the moment when everyone recognized Rachel, when they discovered the drama unfolding in their midst.

"Kat," he said again, stepping closer, trying to keep

this horrible, awkward conversation between the two of them.

"Leave me alone!" Kat jerked her arm up, pushing his away. The contact hurt, but not nearly as much as the desolate look in her eyes.

"Hey, buddy." Brandon's voice floated across the playground as his cousin jogged up to his side. "What's going on?"

"Nothing," Rye said tersely. Kat turned away, trying to hide her tear-streaked face. He took a step to close the new distance between them. Before he could say anything, though, Brandon's fingers closed on his biceps.

"Rye," Brandon said. "Buddy—"

"Leave me alone, *buddy*." He jerked his arm away, letting some of his frustration curl his fingers into fists. "Kat and I are just talking."

"It doesn't look like Kat wants to talk right now." Brandon pitched his voice low.

"Kat—" Rye appealed.

"Please," she said through her tears. "Just leave me alone. I don't want to hear anymore. I can't think about this right now."

"Kat—" he tried one more time.

Brandon shouldered between them. "Come on, buddy—"

Hopeless, helpless anger flashed crimson across Rye's vision. Anger with Brandon, for acting like the town sheriff. Anger with himself, for hurting Kat so deeply. Anger with Rachel, for dragging him into this entire ridiculous mess so long ago, for avoiding his calls until she could inflict maximum damage here, today.

Rye turned on his heel and strode across the park, making his way past the laughing children and their naive game of rescuing the princess. He barely resisted the urge to shout at them, to tell them that the princess was never going to be rescued. The princess was lost forever.

Chapter Nine

Kat felt everyone's eyes turn toward her as Rye stalked off. Brandon took a step closer, asking, "Are you all right?"

"I'm fine," she said, knowing she was lying. How much did he know? How much had he overheard of her fight with Rye?

Her cousin Amanda appeared out of nowhere. "Kat!" Amanda's eyes slid over to Rachel, to the still-cowering Niffer. "What's going on? Are you okay?"

"I'm fine," she repeated, looking around for an escape, knowing that she had to get away from everyone. Amanda seemed to be the Pied Piper; half of Eden Falls followed behind her. A couple of people called out to Rachel, welcoming her home. A few more hollered for Susan and Mike to join the crowd. Kat looked at the sea of faces, and she felt like she was going to faint.

Susan took one glance at her daughters and set her

lips in a grim line. "Rachel," she said, and then she reached out for Kat. "Come sit down, baby. You look like you've seen a ghost! We're all worried about you."

Baby. That was what Rachel called her daughter. Called *Rye's* daughter. One more time, Kat said, "I'm fine." When it was obvious that no one believed her, she looked her mother right in the eye. "Did you know?"

"Know what?" Susan honestly looked perplexed.

"About Rye and Rachel. About Niffer." Kat watched the crowd jostle closer. She imagined the whispers that were even now skating away to those out of earshot. The scandal would be front-page news in seconds.

Susan said, "Dear, I don't know what you're talking about." Even as her kindly face registered concern, though, Kat read sudden comprehension in her eyes. There. Every single person in Eden Falls would add one and one together. They would all know how Kat had been deceived.

Kat pushed away her mother's fluttering hands. "I have to go, Mama."

"Where?"

"I don't know. I just have to get out of here."

Susan looked around helplessly. "Let me get your father—"

"No, you stay with Daddy. And Niffer, too. And Rachel." She practically spat her sister's name.

Susan sounded panicked as she said, "I don't want you going off on your own, dear. You've had a terrible shock. Amanda can—"

"No!" Kat heard the anguish in her voice, and she knew she shouldn't be shouting at her mother, shouldn't take her anger and pain out on an innocent victim. There had been enough innocent victims this spring—herself and Niffer heading up the list. But Kat couldn't hand herself over to Amanda's solicitous care. She couldn't face her cousin's concerned look, her certain questions. Not when Amanda knew so much already. Not when Amanda had been there, the night that Kat and Rye first… She forbade herself to think about that night, to think about the couch, to think about the white-hot heat that had… Forcing her voice to a quieter register, Kat said, "I'm fine, Mama. I just need to get away from here."

And then, because she knew she could not hold back the fresh tears, because she knew she could not bear the pitying looks of the crowd, because she knew she did not have the first idea of what she could ever say or do to make everything—anything—right again, Kat turned on her heel and strode across the park.

She surprised herself by arriving at the parking lot. Rye's truck hulked in a nearby spot, gleaming silver in the bright afternoon sunlight. And all of a sudden, Kat knew what she had to do.

She glanced at her watch. Half an hour. Plenty of time.

Ignoring the people who must still be staring at her, Kat pulled open the truck's door. His keys were exactly where she expected to find them—on the floor mat, just where he had dropped them the night he took her out to the diner. The night he brought her home. The night he fooled her into thinking she was special to him, that they had shared something beautiful and meaningful and unique.

Her mind was filled with memories of Rye. The weight of him, settling over her. The heat of his mouth on hers. The wild passion that he had stroked to life between her thighs. The crashing release that he had given her, the bonds that had pulled them closer to each other.

Or so she had thought.

Her fingers trembled as she picked up the keys. Even as she wanted to block Rye's voice from her memory forever, she heard him instructing her. Foot on the brake. Key in the ignition. Turn the key. Shift into Drive.

Before, when she had driven the truck, she had been haunted by all the things that could go wrong. She had cringed at every sound, shied away from every fast motion.

This time, she did not care. She did not worry about damaging the vehicle, about embarrassing herself in front of the patient man who had sat in the passenger's seat. She did not think about what it meant to conquer a simple summit, the sort of responsibility that nearly every person she knew had accomplished when they were mere teenagers, when they only *thought* they were burdened by all the cares in the world.

Remembering Rye's instruction, Kat looked left, then right, then left again. She shifted her foot off the brake, fully ready when the truck's massive engine began to pull it forward. She gripped the wheel and drove the pickup out of the parking lot.

Afterward, she could not have said how many stop signs she confronted. She could not have told whether the single traffic light was red or green. She could not recount how many trucks she passed, or how many passed her. She only knew that she drove the pickup to the train station, to the empty asphalt patch where her homecoming had begun, a month before.

Was it only a month? Kat felt as if she'd changed so much. When she had arrived in Eden Falls, she had been bound by her lifelong mantra—goals, strategies, rules. The *rules* especially—she'd had one for every situation. She'd known what to expect of herself, of others.

But in one short month, she'd discovered a new way of living. A way that included Magic Zoo and ice cream and late-night bacon blue cheeseburgers and glasses of beer swilled at an actual roadside bar. What had Susan said? That she wanted to see Kat embrace her impulsive side. Well, here was impulse, all right. Let Susan and Mike and Rye and Rachel settle everything, after Kat was back in New York. They'd work it out between them.

Kat shifted the truck into Park and dropped the keys on the floor mat. Entering the tiny station building, she immediately realized she was alone—no one to sell her a ticket. That was fine. She could buy one on the train.

Kat patted the tiny purse that swung from her shoulder. She had bought it when she splurged on her green blouse—was it only the day before? She'd somehow thought she'd been changing herself, remaking herself so that she could live in Eden Falls for the rest of her life.

Ironic, wasn't it? Kat had finally realized she could stay in Eden Falls, work beside her mother at the Morehouse Dance Academy, teach the Advanced Showcase class, and *be happy,* maybe for the first time in years.

But that was before the *Family* Day picnic. That was before she'd learned the truth about her family. About her sister and the man that Kat had come to love.

No. She couldn't say that. Couldn't believe it. She could not love Rye. Not after what he'd done. Not after the secret he had kept from her. Sure, he might only have known that he was Niffer's father for a week. But he had known that he'd slept with Rachel long before that. Slept with her, and kept the truth from Kat. Slept with her, and minimized the connection, made it sound casual, like nothing more than a meaningless fling.

No. She could not love Rye.

She had only *thought* she loved him. She'd been deceived. Rye had presented himself under false pretenses. Whatever emotions Kat thought she had felt were lies. Lies, like his silence had been.

She couldn't sit still on the station's hard wooden bench. She needed to pace, needed to shed some of the physical energy that still sparked through her. She wrapped her arms around her belly and measured out her steps, planting her heels as firmly as if she'd never been hampered by a walking boot.

She should call Haley. Let her roommate know she was coming back to their apartment. Kat was going to make the midnight deadline for the *Coppelia* sign-up after all. She was returning to her life as a dancer.

Forget about *fun*. Dance was her career.

And all that justifying she had done before, all the ways she had convinced herself that Eden Falls was right for her? That was just Kat's tactic for grappling with fear, just like she'd suffered from homesickness, years before, when she'd first moved to New York. She had been *afraid* to reach out for the role she really wanted. She had abandoned her goals, slashed through her strategies, trampled every one of her rules. All because she was afraid she might not have what it took to dance Swanilda.

What had Rye said to her, the day she ran his truck into the ditch? She had to get back on the horse that had thrown her? She had refused then, but she was never going to back down again. Ballet had thrown her, when she developed her stress fracture. Well, it was high time for her to head back to New York. To get back to her real life.

Of course, she didn't have a way to reach Haley. Her cell phone was useless here. And she didn't have any change with her; she couldn't place a call from the ancient pay phone in the corner.

What did it matter, though? She had a credit card; she could buy her train ticket north. And once she got back to the city, she had an apartment full of belongings.

Kat paced some more. This was what Susan had hoped for, wasn't it? That Kat would cast off all bonds, all limits. Susan just hadn't realized that her daughter would use her hard-won freedom to return to New York, without planning, without luggage, without restraint.

She crossed to the wall of windows and pushed her cheek against the glass to peer down the long line of tracks. No train in sight yet. She glanced at her watch. Five minutes.

A strong breeze gusted through the station as the far door opened and someone stepped inside.

When had she learned to recognize the sound of Rye's footsteps? She knew he was standing behind her. She could hear him breathing. She knew that he swallowed hard. She could imagine him reaching toward her, flexing his hands, letting his empty fists fall to his sides.

"Kat," he said. "Please."

She breathed in deeply, as if the gesture could pour steel down her spine, could give her the strength to withstand the next five minutes, until the Clipper chugged into the station. Setting her jaw so that she couldn't possibly say the wrong thing, she turned to face him.

Rye marveled at the change that had come over Kat in the four weeks since they had last been at the train station. Then, she had been a frigid woman, desperate to control the world around her, iced over with frozen fury at the dancer's body that had failed her. Now, he saw a passionate creature, someone who embraced challenge and battled it on her own ground. He had seen her consumed by passion, not just beneath his fingers, not just in response to his lips, but in the very way she tackled living every day.

He had tested a hundred conversational openings on the way from the park, so intent on finding the words to keep Kat in Eden Falls that he nearly crashed his brother Noah's sports car a dozen times. He thought he had worked out the perfect plea, but now all those eloquent words fled him. He was reduced to repeating the only thing that mattered: "Kat, please. Don't leave me."

She glanced at her watch.

He was afraid to check his own, afraid to discover how little time was left for him to plead his case. Instead, he took advantage of her silence, spinning out all the things he'd meant to tell her, all the confessions he'd longed to make. "I know it seems like I deceived you. Hell, I *did* deceive you. And I can't imagine how I've made you feel. But you have to understand—I didn't know. Not until I saw Josh Barton in Richmond. I've spent the past week trying to find Rachel and ask her if it was true. Trying to figure out the right way to tell you. Trying to figure out all the right words."

"But you didn't tell me. Rachel did."

She spoke so quietly that he almost missed her

words. She directed her speech to the knot of her fingers, white-knuckled across her flat belly.

Nevertheless, he took heart that she had said *something*. If she was willing to spare him any words at all, that meant they were having a conversation. They were still communicating. The door between them was still open, even if he could barely make out a glimmer of light on her side.

Even though he knew he was fighting against time, even though he was certain the hourglass was draining away, he chose his words carefully. "I wish it hadn't happened that way. I wish I had told you the second that Josh walked away, in Richmond. I wish I had taken out my phone, dialed your number and told you everything, all at once."

She did not seem to hear him. Instead, she looked around the train station, like a woman in a trance. "Did you know it was me that first day? Did you think I was Rachel?"

This time, she met his eyes. Her silver gaze was cloudy, shrouded in misery. He heard the tremble behind her words, knew she was questioning the very foundation of everything they'd had together.

He held her gaze and answered slowly, setting every syllable between them like an offering on an altar. "I could never confuse the two of you. Ever. You are so much more than the color of your hair and eyes, the shape of your face. Kat, think back to that day. *I* was the one who called out to you, across the parking lot. I knew who you were, even when you pretended not to recognize me."

She had done that, hadn't she? She had played a child's game, because she was afraid of getting caught in a woman's world. And here she was, more tangled than she'd ever thought she could be.

She thought back to the day she had arrived in town, on that unseasonably warm afternoon, with the heat shimmering off the asphalt parking lot. Then, she had thought she would melt. Now, she feared she would never be warm again. She rubbed at her arms and said, "But after that. When you started seeing me with Niffer. There must have been some part of you that knew. You must have wanted me to be Rachel, to be the woman you'd already slept with. You must have wanted us to be the family that the three of you never were."

The words ate through to the core of her heart. In all her life, she had never been jealous of Rachel. Frustrated, yes. Angry with her poor choices. Disappointed by all the times she had made promises, all the times she had lied.

But this was the first time that Kat had ever truly envied her sister. The first time she had ever wanted to change places, to *be* Rachel. Then she would have known what it was like to be the Morehouse sister Rye first made love to. To be the twin he had first chosen. To be the woman he had been drawn to from the start. If Kat had been Rachel, she never would have let Rye out of her sight.

"No," he said, and it seemed like he was damning every one of her dreams. "Kat, I never wanted you to be anyone but who you are. Don't you understand? I never loved Rachel. I'm ashamed to admit this, but I barely *knew* her. She came to me when I had just graduated from college. She'd been dating one of my fraternity brothers. She wanted to make him jealous. I was flattered and stupid and a little naive. I only knew her for a few weeks, but I think I believed that I could...save her. That I could…I don't know…make her be happy and healthy and whole."

Kat *did* know. She knew how many times she had hoped that she could reach out to her twin. How many times Rachel had manipulated Kat's own emotions, making her believe that *this* time things were different, that *this* time Rachel had changed, that *this* time she would be able to hold it all together.

Still, there was more to Rye's story than that.

"Even if I accept that," she said. "Even if I believe every word you've said about what happened six years ago, that doesn't explain now. It doesn't justify your keeping things secret for the past week. You could have called me, any night. You could have told me everything."

Rye heard the sob that cut short her anguish. And yet, that anguish gave him another faint glimmer of hope. If Kat truly hated him, if she were willing to walk away forever, she'd be speaking with more rage. With less conflict. With more of her famed commitment, holding true to the single path she had chosen.

But even as he told himself that all was not absolutely, irrevocably lost, he heard another sound—one that made his pulse quicken with fear. The train whistle keened as the Clipper neared the station. He was almost out of time.

"Kat," he said, certain she heard it, too. "You have to believe me. I never thought of Rachel when I was with you. I kissed your lips, not hers. I touched your body, not hers. In my mind, you are completely separate people. Two women so different that I can only wonder at the coincidence that you're sisters."

She shook her head, using the motion to pull her

around, to face the windows, the train tracks. The door that would carry her out of his life forever.

He knew that he could not touch her, that he could not rely on the incredible physical spark that had joined them, ever since she first returned to Eden Falls. But he could not let her walk away, either, not without making his last argument. Not without saying the words that had pounded through his head as he completed his breakneck drive from the park.

"Kat, I love you. Please. Don't get on that train."

Kat felt the change in air pressure as the locomotive blew past the station door. The train was braking; metal wheels squealed against the track as it came to a stop.

But those sounds meant nothing to her. Instead, she was trapped by the words Rye had spoken. "What did you say?" she asked, her own question almost lost in the station's dead air.

He took a step closer to her. "Kat, I love you." He glanced at the door, at the train that was almost completely stopped. "I love you, and I don't want you to go. I can't get enough of you. I want you to stay here. I *need* you to stay here. But if you can't, if you won't, then I'll get on that train with you. I'll travel to New York, or to anywhere else you go, until I know that you heard me, that you understand me, that you believe me. I love you, Kat Morehouse, and I don't want to live another day without you."

The train was ticking, temporarily settling its weight on the tracks. A conductor walked by on the short platform outside the station, calling out his bored afternoon chant: "Yankee Clipper, all aboard!"

"Kat," Rye whispered, and now he took a step closer. He held out his hand to her, as if she were a forest animal, some shy creature that he had to charm to safety.

He had hurt her. He had kept a terrible secret for days, long past the time when he should speak.

But hadn't she done the very same thing? Hadn't she kept a secret from her mother, hiding the bad news about the studio's bank account because she could not find the right words? Because it was never the right time to tell the truth?

Susan had forgiven her. Susan had told her that she understood—good motives sometimes led to bad actions. All unwitting, Susan had shown Kat the path to understanding. The way to move forward from a bad situation to one that was so much better.

The train seemed to sigh, grumbling as its engine shifted forward. The cars dragged on the track as if they were reluctant to leave Eden Falls. Kat could still run for the Clipper. With her dancer's grace, she could grab hold of the steel grip beside the stairs. She could pull herself into the vestibule, make her way down the swaying, accelerating car to an overpadded seat that would carry her all the way to New York.

But Rye's eyes were pleading with her. Those ebony eyes, darker than any she had ever seen before. No, that was a lie. Niffer's eyes were just as dark.

The train picked up speed. Its whistle blew as the engine rounded the long curve that would bring it north, to Richmond, to Washington, to New York.

The Clipper was gone.

"Thank you," Rye breathed. He was frozen, though, terrified of upsetting the balance he had somehow found, the miracle that had kept Kat in Eden Falls. His hand remained outstretched, his fingers crooked, as if they could remember the cashmere touch of her hair.

"Oh, Rye," she sighed. "I love you, too."

And then, impossibly, she was placing her hand in his. She was letting him pull her close, letting him fold his arms around her. She turned up her face, and he found the perfect offering of her lips.

He wanted to drink all that she had to give him, wanted to sweep her up in his arms and carry her over the threshold of the station, out to Noah's car, and away, far away, into a perfect sunset. He wanted to stay absolutely still, to turn to stone with this incredible woman in his arms, to spin out this moment forever. He wanted to drag her to the hard wooden bench in the center of the waiting room, to pull her down on top of him, to rip open the buttons on her spring-green blouse and lave her perfect breasts with his ever-worshipful tongue.

He wanted to lead Kat, to follow her, to be with her forever.

"Rye." She said his name again, when he finally pulled back from his chaste kiss of promise. There was so much she needed to say to him. So much she needed to hear him say. She twined her fingers in his and led him out of the waiting room, to the glinting form of his silver truck. He barely left her for long enough to walk around the cab to the driver's seat.

As he closed the door behind himself, she felt an eagerness shoot through his body, the need to confirm that she was still beside him, that she had not left him, that she never would. His fingers splayed wide across the back of her head as he pulled her close; urgency sparked from his palm like an actual electric fire. Now his lips were harsh on hers, demanding, and she might have thought that he was angry, if not for the sob that she heard at the back of his throat.

She answered his desperation with need of her own.

Her hands needed to feel the hard muscle of his back. Her arms needed to arch around his chest, to pull him close, closer than she had ever been in any pas de deux.

His clever lips found the fire banked at the base of her throat; his tongue flicked against that delicate hollow until she moaned. By then, his fingers had made their way beneath her blouse; he was doing devastating things to the single clasp of her bra.

Her own hands weren't to be outdone. She flashed through the simple mechanics of releasing his belt, loosening the leather to reach the line of worn buttons beneath. She slid the fingers of her left hand inside the waistband of his jeans as she worked, and she laughed at the feel of his flesh leaping beneath her touch.

But then, three buttons away from freedom, she paused. She flattened her palm against the taut muscles of his belly, pushing away enough that she could see his eyes.

His heartbeat pounded beneath her touch like a wild animal's, and she felt the whisper of his breath, panting as he restrained himself, as he held back for her. "What are we doing, Rye?"

"If you don't know, then I haven't been doing it right," he growled.

She smiled, but she pulled even farther away. She took advantage of his frustrated whimper to tug her blouse back into place. She ran a hand through her hair, forcing it out of her eyes. "I'm serious," she said, and she was pleased to see his hunger take a backseat to concern. "You're living in Richmond now. You've started your own business and you don't have time to do anything new. You don't need the stress of a new relationship, just as you're finally achieving all your dreams."

He caught her hand and planted a kiss in her palm before lacing his fingers between hers. "You *are* all my dreams."

She laughed softly, but she shook her head. "You can say that now, and you probably even believe it. But what are you going to say next week? Next month? Next year? What are you going to say when I keep you from landing the biggest contract you've ever tried for?"

"That's not going to happen," he vowed.

"It will. Rye, I can see a life for myself in Eden Falls. I think a part of me has seen it from the moment I walked into my parents' home. That's why I delayed getting back to New York, why I delayed signing up for the *Coppelia* audition. My body was telling me something when I broke my foot. It knew the truth before my mind did. Before my heart did. Here in Eden Falls, I can help Daddy with his physical therapy, his rehab. I can help Mama at the studio, take over more of the business side of things, teach a few of the classes. I can keep Niffer with me, help her through the pain when she realizes that Rachel is heading out again. We both know my sister will never stick around."

Rye started to tense when Kat said her sister's name. There was no rancor, though, when she spoke of her twin. Only a matter-of-fact acceptance, with just a twinge of sadness for the woman that Rachel might have been.

He used his free hand to brush back Kat's midnight hair. He wanted to make sure she could read his expression when he spoke to her. He wanted to be certain she knew he spoke the truth. "I don't need Richmond."

"But you—"

He cut her off by shaking his head. "Richmond is

just a place. It's not the magical answer to my problems. It's not the secret to the life I wanted to lead."

"Wanted? I don't understand. What was that life?"

"I wanted to be free. I wanted to be independent. I was tired of being everyone's brother, everyone's cousin, everyone's son. I wanted to make my own decisions, to grow my own business, without constantly turning aside to meet someone else's expectation."

"A-and now?" He heard the hesitation in her voice, the tendril of fear behind her question.

"And now, I *want* to be tied to someone else. To *one* someone else. To you. I want to go to work every morning, knowing I'm the best damned contractor I can be. And I want to come home every night, knowing I'm the best husband I can be." He saw her register his words, saw her amazing silver eyes widen in disbelief. "Marry me, Kat. Make me the happiest man in Eden Falls."

Marry him? Marry Rye Harmon?

Kat started to laugh, a shaky sound that mixed suspiciously with a sob in the back of her throat. "I—" she started to say, but then she gave up on that answer. "You—" She trailed off, as if she could not remember how to shape any words.

He chuckled. "I take it that means yes?"

She stared at him—at the good humor that twitched his lips into a smile. At the confidence that squared his shoulders. At the power that rippled down his arms, in the strength of his cunning fingers. At the man who had seen her heart and understood her soul, who knew who she was, and what she needed to be.

"Yes," she said. "Yes, Rye Harmon, I'll marry you."

His kiss was long and deep and satisfying. He was laughing, though, as he pulled away. "You do realize that we have to get back to the park. Everyone is going to be waiting there, worried."

She quirked a grin. There'd be time enough to follow up on the promise of that last kiss. "We can't have that, now, can we?"

She started to reach for her seat belt, but he shook his head. "Not so fast!" he taunted.

"What?"

"I drove Noah's car over here. You're going to have to drive this thing back to the park." He scooped up the keys from the floor mat and pressed them into her yielding palm. "Go ahead," he said, darting in for a quick kiss. "You lead. I'll follow."

Confident that Rye was with her—would be with her forever—she barely glanced in the rearview mirror as she pulled out of the parking lot.

Epilogue

Kat stood at the stove, flexing her ankles and testing her balance as she dropped biscuit dough into a pot of stewed chicken. The motion reminded her of the exercises she had led for the Advanced Showcase students, just that afternoon. The girls had outdone themselves at the barre. In fact, little Taylor Sutton might be ready to audition for the National come spring, if she continued to work hard under Kat's watchful eyes. And, of course, if she wanted to travel so far away from home.

A gust of wind rattled the windows, and Kat peered out at the gathering winter storm. She was glad Rye had installed the new storm windows. For that matter, it was a good thing he'd anchored all the shutters, as well.

"Niffer," Rye said in the living room. "If you don't bring your dolls in from the front yard, they'll have snow on them in the morning."

"I'll get them after dinner," the headstrong child said.

"Now." Rye's calm order made it clear he would brook no disobedience.

"Mommy wouldn't make me bring in my dolls."

"Mommy isn't here, though, is she?" Rye's voice stayed even. He was merely stating a fact. Rachel wasn't there, hadn't been for months. She hadn't even sent a postcard since...when was it? Halloween? "Niffer," Rye said, making it clear that he was through with petulant games. "Let's go. You don't want dinner to be late—Aunt Kat is making your favorite."

The child trotted over to the door, suddenly content to have lost the round. "Okay, Daddy."

Kat shivered and dropped in another dumpling. She couldn't say if her sudden shudder was a reaction to cold air wafting in the house's front door or the sudden proximity of her husband. Rye's hands closed over her belly, and he pulled her back against his chest, nuzzling her neck until she squirmed even closer.

"Good job, Mr. Harmon," she said, after she had caught her breath. "The way to a child's heart is through her stomach."

"Is *that* the secret, Mrs. Harmon?" His teasing fingers strayed to the neckline of her cobalt-blue sweater. "What do you think it would take to convince Niffer to spend the rest of the evening playing in the basement?"

She laughed and arched against him. "We don't have a basement."

"Damn." He switched his attention to the waistline of her pants, dancing around her hips with enough intensity that she had to suck in a steadying breath. "Do you think she could build herself one? Just for tonight? Even for an hour or two?"

Kat set down the wooden spoon she was using to

form the dumplings, and then she twisted in the circle of his arms. She started to fiddle with the top button of his shirt, amazed as always that he didn't need a sweater in the winter cold. "I've been meaning to talk to you about that."

"About Niffer building a basement?" He started to laugh.

"About you building onto the house," she clarified. "I've been thinking we can close in the carport. Convert it into a third bedroom."

She watched as he considered her suggestion. She saw him contemplate the work, solve the engineering problems, determine the most efficient way to add walls, to move doors. And then she saw him register the true meaning behind her suggestion. His fingers tightened deliciously on her waist.

"Really?" he asked, and there was so much love in the word, so much joy, that she found herself laughing out loud.

"Really," she said. His lips on hers were trembling, as if he were suddenly afraid of hurting her. She wasn't about to put up with that—not for eight more months. She cupped her hand on the back of his neck and tugged him closer, making sure she emphasized the demand with a sudden, quick thrust of her tongue.

"When?" he asked as he came up for air.

"Late August, I think. I haven't been to see the doctor yet."

"See the doctor for what?" Niffer's question came from the doorway, tiny and scared.

Kat whirled toward her niece, automatically kneeling to put herself at the child's eye level. "It's okay, sweetheart. No one's sick. I was just telling Daddy that we're going to have a baby join us next summer."

Niffer's eyes grew as big as pie plates. "Will it be a boy baby or a girl baby?"

"I don't know yet," Kat answered gravely. "Which do you want?"

Niffer thought for a long time, and then she said, "One of each."

Kat and Rye laughed at the same time. "Maybe we'll just take things one step at a time," Rye said, ruffling his daughter's hair. "Come on, now. Help me set the dinner table."

Kat was still grinning as Niffer hurried to grab the silverware out of its drawer. Girl or boy, it didn't matter to her—so long as everyone was healthy and happy and safe in Eden Falls.

* * * * *

HEART & HOME

Heartwarming romances where love can
happen right when you least expect it.

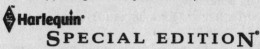

COMING NEXT MONTH
AVAILABLE JANUARY 31, 2012

#2167 FORTUNE'S VALENTINE BRIDE
The Fortunes of Texas: Whirlwind Romance
Marie Ferrarella

#2168 THE RETURN OF BOWIE BRAVO
Bravo Family Ties
Christine Rimmer

#2169 JACKSON HOLE VALENTINE
Rx for Love
Cindy Kirk

#2170 A MATCH MADE BY CUPID
The Foster Brothers
Tracy Madison

#2171 ALMOST A HOMETOWN BRIDE
Helen R. Myers

#2172 HIS MOST IMPORTANT WIN
Cynthia Thomason

You can find more information on upcoming Harlequin® titles,
free excerpts and more at www.HarlequinInsideRomance.com.

HSECNM0112

REQUEST YOUR FREE BOOKS!

2 FREE NOVELS PLUS 2 FREE GIFTS!

SPECIAL EDITION

Life, Love & Family

YES! Please send me 2 FREE Harlequin® Special Edition novels and my 2 FREE gifts (gifts are worth about $10). After receiving them, if I don't wish to receive any more books, I can return the shipping statement marked "cancel." If I don't cancel, I will receive 6 brand-new novels every month and be billed just $4.49 per book in the U.S. or $5.24 per book in Canada. That's a saving of at least 14% off the cover price! It's quite a bargain! Shipping and handling is just 50¢ per book in the U.S. and 75¢ per book in Canada.* I understand that accepting the 2 free books and gifts places me under no obligation to buy anything. I can always return a shipment and cancel at any time. Even if I never buy another book, the two free books and gifts are mine to keep forever.

235/335 HDN FEGF

Name	(PLEASE PRINT)

Address	Apt. #

City	State/Prov.	Zip/Postal Code

Signature (if under 18, a parent or guardian must sign)

Mail to the **Reader Service:**
IN U.S.A.: P.O. Box 1867, Buffalo, NY 14240-1867
IN CANADA: P.O. Box 609, Fort Erie, Ontario L2A 5X3

Not valid for current subscribers to Harlequin Special Edition books.

Want to try two free books from another line?
Call 1-800-873-8635 or visit www.ReaderService.com.

* Terms and prices subject to change without notice. Prices do not include applicable taxes. Sales tax applicable in N.Y. Canadian residents will be charged applicable taxes. Offer not valid in Quebec. This offer is limited to one order per household. All orders subject to credit approval. Credit or debit balances in a customer's account(s) may be offset by any other outstanding balance owed by or to the customer. Please allow 4 to 6 weeks for delivery. Offer available while quantities last.

Your Privacy—The Reader Service is committed to protecting your privacy. Our Privacy Policy is available online at www.ReaderService.com or upon request from the Reader Service.

We make a portion of our mailing list available to reputable third parties that offer products we believe may interest you. If you prefer that we not exchange your name with third parties, or if you wish to clarify or modify your communication preferences, please visit us at www.ReaderService.com/consumerschoice or write to us at Reader Service Preference Service, P.O. Box 9062, Buffalo, NY 14269. Include your complete name and address.

Discover a touching new trilogy from
USA TODAY bestselling author

Janice Kay Johnson

Between Love and Duty

As the eldest brother of three, Duncan MacLachlan
is used to being in control and maintaining an
emotional distance; as a police captain it's his job.
But when he meets Jane Brooks, Duncan soon finds
his control slipping away. Together, they fight for a
young boy's future, and soon Duncan finds himself
hoping to build a future with Jane.

Available February 2012

From Father to Son
(March 2012)

The Call of Bravery
(April 2012)

www.Harlequin.com

HSR71758

Louisa Morgan loves being around children.
So when she has the opportunity to tutor bedridden Ellie,
she's determined to bring joy back into the motherless
girl's world. Can she also help Ellie's father open his
heart again? Read on for a sneak peek of

THE COWBOY FATHER

by Linda Ford,
available February 2012 from Love Inspired Historical.

Why had Louisa thought she could do this job? A bubble of self-pity whispered she was totally useless, but Louisa ignored it. She wasn't useless. She could help Ellie if the child allowed it.

Emmet walked her out, waiting until they were out of earshot to speak. "I sense you and Ellie are not getting along."

"Ellie has lost her freedom. On top of that, everything is new. Familiar things are gone. Her only defense is to exert what little independence she has left. I believe she will soon tire of it and find there are more enjoyable ways to pass the time."

He looked doubtful. Louisa feared he would tell her not to return. But after several seconds' consideration, he sighed heavily. "You're right about one thing. She's lost everything. She can hardly be blamed for feeling out of sorts."

"She hasn't lost everything, though." Her words were quiet, coming from a place full of certainty that Emmet was more than enough for this child. "She has you."

"She'll always have me. As long as I live." He clenched his fists. "And I fully intend to raise her in such a way that even if something happened to me, she would never feel like I was gone. I'd be in her thoughts and in her actions every day."

Peace filled Louisa. "Exactly what my father did."

Their gazes connected, forged a single thought about fathers and daughters…how each needed the other. How sweet the relationship was.

Louisa tipped her head away first. "I'll see you tomorrow."

Emmet nodded. "Until tomorrow then."

She climbed behind the wheel of their automobile and turned toward home. She admired Emmet's devotion to his child. It reminded her of the love her own father had lavished on Louisa and her sisters. Louisa smiled as fond memories of her father filled her thoughts. Ellie was a fortunate child to know such love.

Louisa understands what both father and daughter are going through. Will her compassion help them heal—and form a new family? Find out in
THE COWBOY FATHER
by Linda Ford, available February 14, 2012.

Love Inspired Books celebrates 15 years of inspirational romance in 2012! February puts the spotlight on Love Inspired Historical, with each book celebrating family and the special place it has in our hearts. Be sure to pick up all four Love Inspired Historical stories, available February 14, wherever books are sold.

Copyright © 2012 by Linda Ford

SHLIHEXP0212

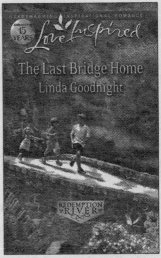

Firefighter Zak Ashford always does the right thing. So when a dying woman from his past asks him to be the guardian to her three troubled children, he accepts. In turmoil, Zak turns to neighbor Jilly Fairmont for help. It isn't long before Zak realizes what Jilly means to him. But can he convince Jilly to be a part of his future?

The Last Bridge Home
by Linda Goodnight

Available February wherever books are sold.

www.LoveInspiredBooks.com

LI87722

USA TODAY bestselling author

Sarah Morgan

brings readers another enchanting story

ONCE A FERRARA WIFE...

When Laurel Ferrara is summoned back to Sicily by her estranged husband, billionaire Cristiano Ferrara, Laurel knows things are about to heat up. And Cristiano's power is a potent reminder of his Sicilian dynasty's unbreakable rule: once a Ferrara wife, always a Ferrara wife....

Sparks fly this February

HP13049